Twelve Years a Slave

U0025452

自由之心

為奴十二年

Twelve Years a Slave

Twelve Years a Slave

原著 _Solomon Northup
改寫 _ David A. Hill
譯者 _ 安卡斯

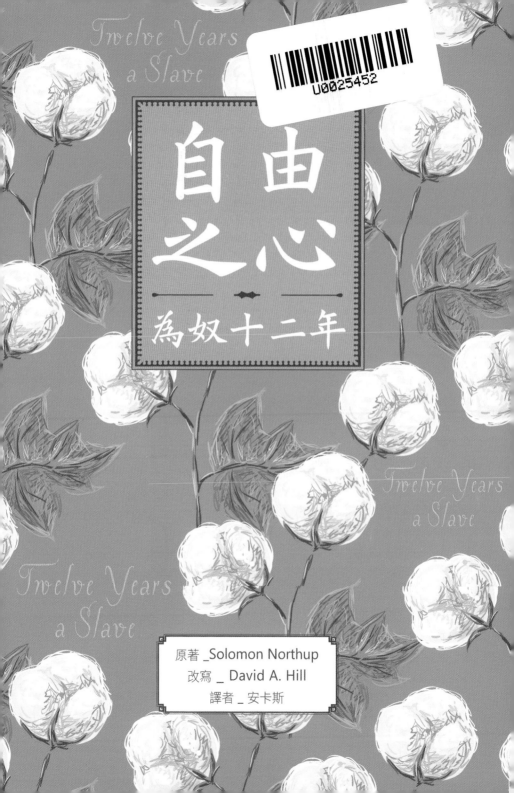

ABOUT THIS BOOK

For the Student

- Listen to the story and do some activities on your Audio CD.
- Talk about the story.
- Prepare for Cambridge English: Preliminary (PET) for schools.

For the Teacher

HELBLING e-ZONE THE EDUCATIONAL PLATFORM A state-of-the-art interactive learning environment with 1000s of free online self-correcting activities for your chosen readers.

Go to our Readers Resource site for information on using readers and downloadable Resource Sheets, photocopiable Worksheets, and Tapescripts.
www.helblingreaders.com

For lots of great ideas on using Graded Readers consult Reading Matters, the Teacher's Guide to using Helbling Readers.

Level 5 Structures

Modal verb would	Non-defining relative clauses
I'd love to . . .	Present perfect continuous
Future continuous	Used to / would
Present perfect future	Used to / used to doing
Reported speech / verbs / questions	Second conditional
Past perfect	Expressing wishes and regrets
Defining relative clauses	

Structures from other levels are also included.

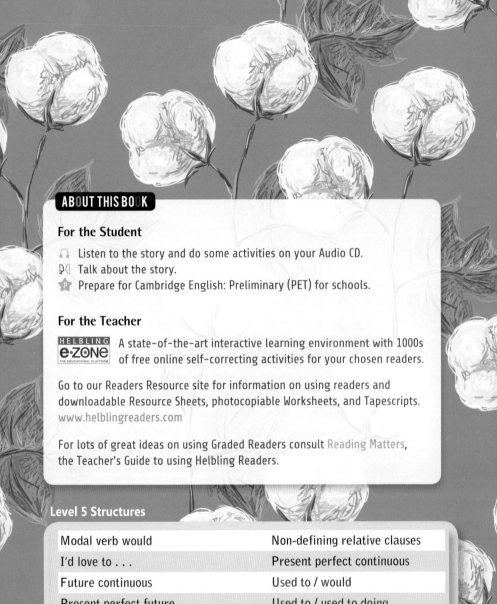

CONTENTS

About the Author

Solomon Northup was born in July 1808 in the state[1] of New York in the USA. His father had originally[2] been a slave[3] for the Northup family, but after years of service, they gave him his freedom[4]. After this Solomon's family—father, mother and elder brother Joseph—moved around the area, as free men doing various kinds of work. Solomon's father made sure that his sons had as good an education as possible.

Solomon married in 1829 and started a family as a free man. But, some years later, while he was looking for[5] work one day, Solomon met two white men, who tricked[6] him and sold him into slavery[7] in Washington. Solomon then lived as a slave

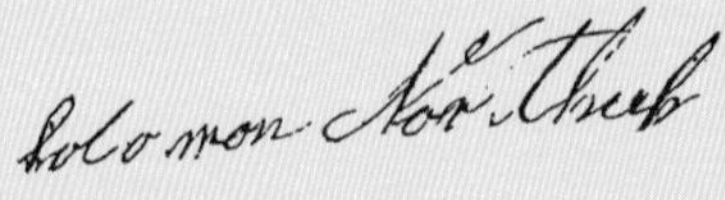

for twelve years until he was rescued[8] by the lawyer Henry B. Northup—from the same family which had freed his father. This book is the story of Solomon Northup's twelve terrible years as a slave.

Slavery in the USA dates back to British colonial[9] times, and was recognized[10] by thirteen states after the Declaration of Independence[11] in 1776. Black people were first brought from Africa to the USA where they were sold as slaves to work on tobacco, sugar and cotton plantations[12] in the slave states. A slave state was a state in which slavery was legal and a free state was one in which slavery was illegal[13]. Slaves had no rights and were seen by their white owners as little more than animals or machines[14]. Slavery was not abolished[15] in all states of the USA until 1865.

1 state [stet] (n.) 州
2 originally [əˋrɪdʒənl̩ɪ] (adv.) 起初；原來
3 slave [slev] (n.) 奴隸
4 freedom [ˋfridəm] (n.) 自由
5 look for 尋找
6 trick [trɪk] (v.) 詐騙
7 slavery [ˋslevərɪ] (n.) 奴隸身分；奴役
8 rescue [ˋrɛskju] (v.) 營救
9 colonial [kəˋlonjəl] (a.) 殖民的
10 recognize [ˋrɛkəg͵naɪz] (v.) 認可
11 Declaration of Independence《美國獨立宣言》
12 plantation [plænˋteʃən] (n.) 農場；耕地
13 illegal [ɪˋlig!] (a.) 非法的
14 machine [məˋʃin] (n.) 機器
15 abolish [əˋbɑlɪʃ] (v.) 廢除；廢止

About the Book

Twelve Years a Slave follows the story of a free man, Solomon Northup, from 1841, when he was illegally sold into slavery, from the initial[1] period as a slave to William Ford, through the increasingly cruel times under John M. Tibeats, and then with Edwin Epps, from whom Solomon was eventually[2] rescued in 1853.

Solomon paints a clear picture of the life of a slave, the endless work and unfair treatment[3], where people are generally treated as property[4], without any humanity[5]. The book gives details of the slaves' daily duties[6], as well as[7] the particular things which happened to Solomon, including his attempts to escape[8].

In May 1853, Solomon Northup published[9] his story. It was edited[10] by David Wilson. Solomon wanted readers to understand the situation[11] of black slaves in the slave states of the USA. In his preface[12], the editor, David Wilson, said that he firmly[13] believed that the story of Solomon's

1 initial [ɪ`nɪʃəl] (a.) 最初的
2 eventually [ɪ`vɛntʃuəlɪ] (adv.) 最後地；終於地
3 treatment [`tritmənt] (n.) 對待
4 property [`prɑpətɪ] (n.) 財產；所有物
5 humanity [hju`mænətɪ] (n.) 人性；人道
6 duty [`djutɪ] (n.) 職責
7 as well as 而且；還
8 escape [ə`skep] (v.) 逃跑；逃脫
9 publish [`pʌblɪʃ] (v.) 出版
10 edit [`ɛdɪt] (v.) 編輯

twelve years of slavery was true. He checked it as far as he could, although it was not possible to get evidence[14] about everything.

Wilson stated that Solomon's "fortune"[15] during his time as a slave, lay in the fact that he was owned by several different masters. Some showed humanity, while others only cruelty[16]. And indeed, Solomon writes of these people with either gratitude[17] or bitterness[18].

In 2012 *Twelve Years a Slave* was made into a film directed by Steve McQueen. It was mostly filmed around New Orleans, Louisiana, in the summer of 2012 using four historic[19] cotton plantations for the location[20]. The film was first released[21] in 2013 and it has won several major awards[22].

11 situation [ˌsɪtʃuˋeʃən] (n.) 情況；處境
12 preface [ˋprɛfɪs] (n.) 序言；前言
13 firmly [ˋfɝmlɪ] (adv.) 堅固地
14 evidence [ˋɛvədəns] (n.) 證據
15 fortune [ˋfɔrtʃən] (n.) 好運；幸運
16 cruelty [ˋkruəltɪ] (n.) 殘酷行為
17 gratitude [ˋgrætəˏtjud] (n.) 感激之情；感恩
18 bitterness [ˋbɪtənɪs] (n.) 痛苦；悲痛
19 historic [hɪsˋtɔrɪk] (a.) 歷史上著名的
20 location [loˋkeʃən] (n.) 場所
21 release [rɪˋlis] (v.) 發行
22 award [əˋwɔrd] (n.) 獎；獎項

Before Reading

1 This story speaks about slavery in the USA. The first African slaves were brought to the USA in 1619 and slavery was legal in many states until its abolition in 1865. Look at the picture and definition and tick (✓) the words you feel are associated with slavery from the list below. Explain your choices to a friend. Use a dictionary if necessary.

> **Slavery** is the act of buying and selling people. A person becomes the property of another person.

- ☐ abolish
- ☐ chains
- ☐ comfortable
- ☐ freedom
- ☐ happy
- ☐ holiday
- ☐ owner
- ☐ work
- ☐ punishment
- ☐ rights
- ☐ legal property

2 Use some of the words from Exercise **1** to complete these sentences from the story.

a) He didn't think of the black man as a human being but as a piece of living ______.

b) I was alone, in complete darkness and in ______.

c) He shouted that if I ever said I was a free man again, or that I had been kidnapped, I would receive even worse ______.

d) Some talked of escape but feared the consequences if they were caught and then had to return to their ______.

3 The slaves in the story are transported from Washington to New Orleans. Match the correct means of transport with the pictures.

1) steamboat 2) on foot
3) sailing ship 4) wagon

a 

b 

c 

d 

4 Use the words from Exercise **3** to complete the sentences.

(a) We started our long journey on a ____________ traveling down the Potomac River.

(b) We sailed in a large ____________ on the open sea, down south to New Orleans.

(c) We drove eighteen miles towards Great Pine Woods in a ____________.

(d) We had to walk the last twelve miles ____________.

5 These are some of the places in the story.
Match the word below with a definition in the box.

(1) small simple house
(2) large farm where crops are grown
(3) outside area with walls all around
(4) area of water and mud

____ (a) plantation

____ (b) swamp

____ (c) yard

____ (d) cabin

6 Solomon Northup is the main character and he tells us his own story. Read the extract, look at the picture, and then tick (✓) the correct option below.

Anne and I stayed in Saratoga Springs until early 1841, we were comfortable but not rich, so every opportunity to make more money was important. During this time we had three children – Elizabeth, Margaret and Alonzo – who made us very happy.

a) From this description we understand that Solomon ______.

- ☐ was very poor
- ☐ lived quite well

b) We have the impression that he was ______.

- ☐ a hard worker
- ☐ a lazy person

c) We also understand that he was ______.

- ☐ very ambitious
- ☐ a family man

7 Solomon Northup was born a free man but was kidnapped, taken prisoner and sold as a slave. "Kidnapped" is when a person, not an object, is stolen. Listen to what Solomon says and tick (✓) true (T) or false (F).

T F (a) Solomon thought about his family often.
T F (b) Sometimes he cried.
T F (c) He didn't want to escape. It was too dangerous.
T F (d) He was taken to California.
T F (e) He was given a different name.

8 Match the jobs from the story to the correct definitions.

1. person who works on a farm
2. person who buys and sells slaves
3. person who gathers cotton from the plants
4. person who checks people as they work
5. person who makes things from wood

_____ (a) carpenter
_____ (b) overseer
_____ (c) cotton picker
_____ (d) slave dealer
_____ (e) agricultural worker

9 Solomon had three masters or owners during his twelve years as a slave. Listen to the descriptions of his three masters and tick (✓) if they were "good" or "bad" masters below each name.

a	Ford	☐ good	☐ bad
b	Tibeats	☐ good	☐ bad
c	Epps	☐ good	☐ bad

10 Now listen again and complete their descriptions with the words from the listening.

bad-tempered master drank opposite spoke
religious manners lucky cunning

a William Ford was a very ________ man. He was a good ________ and his slaves were ________ to have him as a master.

b John M. Tibeats, a small, ________, ignorant man who was the complete ________ of Master Ford.

c Edwin Epps ________ in an uneducated way and his ________ were disgusting. He also ________ a lot. He was quiet and ________.

Chapter 1

My origins

5 *My name is Solomon Northup and I was born a free man. I lived free for thirty years, then I was kidnapped[1] and sold as a slave. I lived as a slave for twelve years until I was rescued and again became a free man. This is the story of what happened to me.*

My father was a slave and worked for the Northup family in the state of New York. When old Mr Northup died (around 1800), he gave my father his freedom. My father then took his family name and became Mintus Northup. The Northup family always took an interest in[2] us, and it is because of Henry B. Northup, a famous lawyer and relative of the original Northup family, that I am now free again.

After my father was granted[3] his freedom, he worked on many different farms in New York State doing agricultural[4] work with my mother and my elder brother.

1 kidnap [ˋkɪdnæp] (v.) 綁架
2 take an interest in . . . 對⋯⋯有興趣
3 grant [grænt] (v.) 准予；授予
4 agricultural [ˏægrɪˋkʌltʃərəl] (a.) 農業的

I was born in July 1808. We lived happily together. Because of my father's ideas and teaching, we got a better education than most African Americans.

Our father also often talked to us about his earlier life as a slave. He was never treated badly as a slave but he thought it important for us to understand the system of slavery and what it meant for our people.

I started doing farm work with my father from a young age, but in my free time, I studied, and also played the violin, which was my greatest passion[1]. My father died in 1820.

In 1829 I married Anne Hampton, who was a free woman of mixed origins[2]. I then took a series of different manual[3] jobs to make extra money. These jobs meant I often traveled, and I even visited Canada once.

We eventually had enough money to take a farm and then I started agricultural work. Anne often worked as a cook[4], and I was frequently in demand[5] to play my violin at local dances in the evenings, so for a time we lived comfortably but simply on what we both earned.

In the hope of earning more money, in 1834 we moved to Saratoga Springs, in New York State. I worked as a carriage[6] driver, and Anne cooked at a nearby hotel. I also earned extra money playing the violin, and doing occasional[7] manual work.

1 passion [ˋpæʃən] (n.) 熱情
2 origin [ˋɔrədʒɪn] (n.) 血統
3 manual [ˋmænjuəl] (a.) 體力的
4 cook [kʊk] (n.) 廚師
5 in demand 非常需要的；受歡迎的
6 carriage [ˋkærɪdʒ] (n.) 馬車
7 occasional [əˋkeʒənl̩] (a.) 偶而的

HOTEL

7 During this time, I often met slaves who had traveled from the south with their masters. They were all well dressed and well provided for and seemed to lead a relatively easy life. But after talking with them about their situation I discovered they all wanted to become free men. Some talked of escape but feared[1] the consequences[2] if they were caught and then had to return to their owners.

These conversations made me even more certain of what my father had said about the awful nature[3] of slavery and the need for liberty[4] for all men.

Anne and I stayed in Saratoga Springs until early 1841, we were comfortable but not rich, so every opportunity[5] to make more money was important. During this time we had three children—Elizabeth, Margaret and Alonzo—who made us very happy.

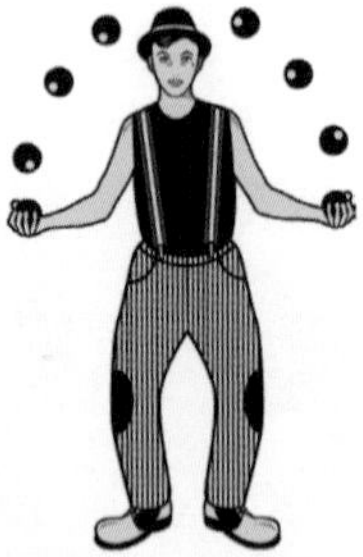

1 fear [fɪr] (v.) 害怕；擔心
2 consequence [ˋkɑnsə͵kwɛns] (n.) 後果
3 nature [ˋnetʃɚ] (n.) 本質
4 liberty [ˋlɪbɚtɪ] (n.) 自由
5 opportunity [͵ɑpɚˋtjunətɪ] (n.) 機會
6 private [ˋpraɪvɪt] (a.) 私人的；私下的
7 offer [ˋɔfɚ] (v.) 提供
8 fare [fɛr] (n.) 交通費用
9 financial [faɪˋnænʃəl] (a.) 財務的
10 note [not] (n.) 便條；短信
11 a change of clothes 一套更換的衣服
12 juggle [ˋdʒʌgl̩] (v.) 耍球把戲
13 ventriloquism [vɛnˋtrɪləkwɪzəm] (n.) 腹語（術）
14 magic trick 魔術把戲
15 badly attended 觀賞的人很少

Chapter 2

Two strangers

8 In March 1841, Anne was away with the children at Sandy Hill, cooking. I was looking for work in Saratoga when I met two well-dressed white men called Hamilton and Brown. They belonged to a circus show, from the city of Washington, and were on a private[6] tour, visiting the area and giving occasional performances. They needed someone to play the music for their show as they traveled to New York, and offered[7] me $1 for each day, with $3 for each performance, and the return fare[8] from New York to Saratoga.

I accepted this good financial[9] offer immediately. Thinking it was only a short trip, I left no note[10] for Anne, and just took my violin and a change of clothes[11].

We traveled to Albany by carriage, arriving in the evening. They performed and I played my violin. Brown juggled[12], danced on a rope, did some ventriloquism[13] and magic tricks[14], while Hamilton stayed at the door. It was very badly attended[15] and made almost no money.

Note

- What do you usually do when you go somewhere? Tick (✓).
  - ☐ Leave a note.
  - ☐ Tell someone.
  - ☐ Send a message.
  - ☐ Phone someone.
- When you go somewhere why is it always a good idea to tell someone where you are going? Discuss with a partner.

9 We left early next morning, and they decided not to do any more performances, but go straight to New York. There, they asked me to go to Washington to join their circus, offering me such good pay that I agreed.

The next day, they suggested I get my "free papers[1]", since Washington was in a slave state. It seemed a sensible[2] idea, so we went to the Customs House[3] and got the documents[4]. Then we traveled to Washington.

Brown and Hamilton were always extremely[5] polite to me, treating me very well. That evening they gave me $43, apologizing[6] for the lack of performances that they had promised.

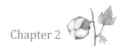

10 They took me to visit the Capitol[7], the President's House[8] and other sights[9]. From time to time, we stopped for a drink, which they always gave me. When we got back to our hotel, I started to feel very ill and was unable to eat dinner. I had a terrible headache, could not sleep and got very thirsty but even water didn't make me feel better.

Slave state

- Find out some information about a "slave state" and a "free state."
- Go back to page 5 for a definition and use the Internet to help you. Discuss in groups.

1 papers [ˋpepɚz] (n.)〔複〕文件
2 sensible [ˋsɛnsəbl̩] (a.) 明智的；合情理的
3 Customs House 海關
4 document [ˋdɑkjəmənt] (n.) 公文；文件
5 extremely [ɪkˋstrimlɪ] (adv.) 極度地
6 apologize [əˋpɑlə͵dʒaɪz] (v.) 道歉
7 Capitol [ˋkæpətəl] (n.) 美國國會大廈
8 President's House 費城總統宮
9 sights [saɪts] (n.)〔複〕觀光地點

11

Later I was told that I needed to visit a doctor. I was led into the street. I have no idea what happened after that.

When I became conscious[1] again I was alone, in complete darkness, and in chains[2]. I felt very weak. I was sitting on a low bench. I had handcuffs[3] on, and there were metal[4] rings round my ankles attached[5] by a chain to a ring in the floor.

I was unable to stand up. Where was I? Where were Brown and Hamilton? Why was I imprisoned[6] like this? I had been robbed of my money and my "free papers". I realized that I must have been kidnapped and felt terribly alone and desperate[7]; I wept[8] bitterly[9].

1 conscious [ˋkɑnʃəs] (a.) 有意識到的
2 chains [tʃenz] (n.)〔複〕枷鎖；鐐銬
3 handcuff [ˋhænd͵kʌf] (n.) 手銬
4 metal [ˋmɛtḷ] (n.) 金屬製品
5 attach [əˋtætʃ] (v.) 繫上；附上
6 imprison [ɪmˋprɪzṇ] (v.) 禁錮
7 desperate [ˋdɛspərɪt] (a.) 絕望的
8 weep [wip] (v.) 哭泣
（三態：weep; wept; wept）
9 bitterly [ˋbɪtəlɪ] (adv.) 痛苦地

Chapter 3

Chains and darkness

12 At some point, the door was opened, and light flooded[1] in the room. I could finally see where I was—a bare[2] cellar[3] with a wooden floor, and the bench I was sitting on.

Two men came into the room: James H. Burch and Ebenezer Radburn. Burch was a large, powerful man of about forty, with a cruel and cunning[4] face. He was a well-known slave dealer[5] in Washington. Radburn was his general[6] assistant[7].

"How do you feel?" asked Burch.

I said I was sick, and asked why I had been imprisoned. He said he had bought me, that I was his slave and he was sending me to New Orleans.

I shouted loudly that I was a free man, a resident[8] of Saratoga, where I had a wife and children and that my name was Northup. He said I was not free, and that I came from Georgia.

Again, I told him that I was free, and ordered him to take off my chains.

He became extremely angry and called me a liar, saying that I was a slave who had run away from his master in Georgia. Burch then ordered Radburn to fetch[9] the paddle[10] and the cat-o'-nine-tails[11].

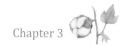

13 The paddle was a wooden board[12]. The cat-o'-nine-tails was a thick rope with many parts, each with a knot tied at the end. Then they undressed[13] me and pulled me across the bench. Burch started beating[14] my body with the paddle. He stopped and asked if I still said I was a free man. I did, and he started again, faster and harder than before.

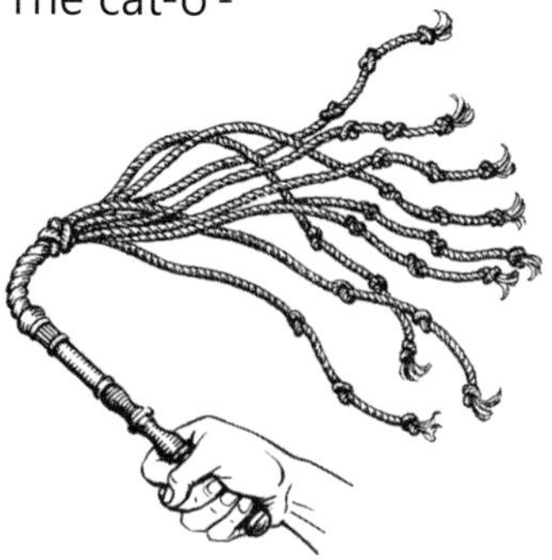

All this happened several more times. In the end, the paddle broke, but he could not force me to say the lie that I was a slave. He then took the cat, and started beating me with that. This was even more painful, and my body felt as if it was on fire and that only my bones remained[15].

Finally Radburn said that more beating was useless and Burch stopped. He shouted that if ever I said I was a free man again, or that I had been kidnapped, I would receive even worse punishment[16]. Then they took the handcuffs off, and went out, locking the door and leaving me in darkness again.

1 flood [flʌd] (v.) 充滿；充斥
2 bare [bɛr] (a.) 空的；無陳設的
3 cellar [ˋsɛlɚ] (n.) 地下室；地窖
4 cunning [ˋkʌnɪŋ] (a.) 狡猾的
5 dealer [ˋdilɚ] (n.) 販子
6 general [ˋdʒɛnərəl] (a.) （職位）總的；首席的
7 assistant [əˋsɪstənt] (n.) 助手
8 resident [ˋrɛzədənt] (n.) 居民
9 fetch [fɛtʃ] (v.) 拿來
10 paddle [ˋpædḷ] (n.) 槳；拍子
11 cat-o'-nine-tails [ˏkætəˋnaɪnˏtelz] (n.) 九尾鞭
12 board [bord] (n.) 木板
13 undress [ʌnˋdrɛs] (v.) 脫下……的衣服
14 beat [bit] (v.) 打 （三態：beat; beat; beat/beaten）
15 remain [rɪˋmen] (v.) 剩下；餘留
16 punishment [ˋpʌnɪʃmənt] (n.) 懲罰

14 Radburn returned later bringing a small piece of fried pork, a slice[1] of bread and a cup of water. He suggested not saying more about being a free man, unless I wanted to be beaten again. He then unlocked the chains on my ankles, opened a little window with bars[2] on it, and left me alone again.

By then I had become very sore[3] and could only move with great pain. That night I lay on the hard, bare floor with no pillow or covering[4].

Imagine

- Can you even imagine how Solomon is feeling?
- What did Brown and Hamilton do to Solomon?

Twice a day, Radburn came in with the same food. I was always thirsty. My wounds[5] did not allow me to remain in any position[6] for long. I thought of my wife and children frequently, which made me weep. But my spirit[7] was still not broken. I thought about ways of escaping. I could not believe that one man could treat another so unjustly[8]. I kept hoping that Burch might release[9] me when he found out that I really was a free man, or that Brown and Hamilton might come looking for me.

15 After a few days, I was allowed out into a yard. There I found three slaves: a boy of ten years and two young men in their twenties. We talked and I learnt a little of how they had come there.

We were all given horse blankets, which was the only bedding[10] I was allowed for the next twelve years.

After two weeks in Williams's slave pen[11]—as this place was called—the boy's mother and sister were also brought in. They were delighted to see each other, though the mother—Eliza—was aware that they might be separated[12] forever.

Association[13]

- Underline the words on this page that are usually associated[14] with animals and not people.
- What does this tell about how these slaves were treated? Discuss in groups.

1 slice [slaɪs] (n.) 薄片
2 bar [bɑr] (n.) 棒；條
3 sore [sor] (a.) 疼痛發炎的
4 covering [ˋkʌvərɪŋ] (n.) 覆蓋物；毯子；被子
5 wound [wund] (n.) 傷口
6 position [pəˋzɪʃən] (n.) 姿勢
7 spirit [ˋspɪrɪt] (n.) 精神；心靈
8 unjustly [ʌnˋdʒʌstlɪ] (adv.) 不義地；不法地
9 release [rɪˋlis] (v.) 釋放；豁免
10 bedding [ˋbɛdɪŋ] (n.) 寢具
11 pen [pɛn] (n.)（關禽畜的）欄；圈
12 separate [ˋsɛpə,ret] (v.) 分隔
13 association [ə,sosɪˋeʃən] (n.) 聯想
14 associate [əˋsoʃɪ,et] (v.) 聯想

Chapter 4

Journey south

16 At midnight one night soon after, Burch and Radburn ordered us to get up and they put us on a steamboat[1]. We were starting our long journey to New Orleans. They pushed us down into the hold[2], and we traveled down the Potomac River. Before noon next day the boat reached Aquia Creek. Burch put us into a wagon[3] with him, and we drove to Richmond, the capital[4] of Virginia. There we were taken to Goodin's slave pen. Burch and Goodin were clearly old friends.

Next afternoon, we all walked in twos[5] through the streets of Richmond to a large sailing ship, the *Orleans*. By then there were forty of us altogether and we were all locked in the hold.

We arrived at the city of Norfolk, where the smaller boat brought four more slaves onto the *Orleans*: two boys, a girl, and a man called Arthur who arrived struggling[6] with his keepers[7], protesting[8] loudly and with a badly beaten face. I later learnt that, like me, he had been a free man, but had been caught by a gang[9] at night in the street and then taken to a slave pen for several days.

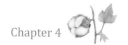

17 Our journey on board was long and we were often sick, because of bad weather, until we passed the Bahama Banks.

One of the men on board with us got ill with smallpox[10] and died before we reached New Orleans. The days passed slowly but we all had jobs to do keeping us busy all day and at night we were all locked up in the hold.

One day a sailor called John Manning talked to me. I explained that I was a free man who had been kidnapped, and he said he wanted to help me. I asked him to find me pen, ink and paper so that I could write a letter to Mr Henry B. Northup asking for help.

So that night I hid under a small boat on the deck[11], met Manning, wrote the letter and gave it to him. He promised to post the letter from New Orleans.

1 steamboat [ˋstimbot] (n.) 汽船
2 hold [hold] (n.) 貨艙
3 wagon [ˋwægən] (n.) 運貨馬車

4 capital [ˋkæpətl̩] (n.) 首府
5 in twos 兩兩；成雙
6 struggle [ˋstrʌgl̩] (v.) 對抗
7 keeper [ˋkipɚ] (n.) 看守人
8 protest [prəˋtɛst] (v.) 抗議
9 gang [gæŋ] (n.) 一幫人
10 smallpox [ˋsmɔl͵pɑks] (n.) 天花
11 deck [dɛk] (n.) 甲板；(車)層

Solomon Northup's
Journey
South
SARATOGA
SPRINGS
NEW
YORK
WASHINGTON
RICHMOND
NORFOLK
NEW
ORLEANS
BAHAMAS

18 I later heard that Mr Northup did receive the letter, and took it to the authorities[1], but because nobody knew where I was exactly, they decided to wait for more information before doing anything.

Arthur, however, had more luck: when we eventually landed in New Orleans, two men came to free him. His kidnappers had been arrested[2], and after talking to the captain, Arthur left the ship with them. I was pleased for him, but this also made me feel even more desperate and alone.

In New Orleans Mr Theophilus Freeman arrived to take Burch's slaves away. At first there was some confusion[3] because he called me by the name of Platt, which is what Burch had told him my name was. And so Platt became the name I was called for the next twelve years as a slave.

We were taken to Freeman's slave pen, which was similar to Goodin's in Richmond.

Next day, Freeman dressed us all in simple, new clothes. Many customers came. They examined[4] us, and Freeman spoke of our good qualities. An old gentleman from New Orleans wanted me as his carriage driver, but he refused[5] to pay the $1,500 Freeman was asking for me.

1 authorities [əˋθɔrətɪz] (n.)〔複〕當局
2 arrest [əˋrɛst] (v.) (n.) 逮捕
3 confusion [kənˋfjuʒən] (n.) 混亂；混淆
4 examine [ɪgˋzæmɪn] (v.) 檢查
5 refuse [rɪˋfjuz] (v.) 拒絕

19 That night, those of us from the *Orleans* were taken[1] ill. I told the doctor about Robert's smallpox. Eliza, her children, a man called Harry and I were taken to a large hospital outside the city. I was very ill, and expected to die. However, I survived and two weeks later, returned to Freeman's pen together with the others. We were much weakened[2] by our illness but now ready to be sold.

Some days later, a well-dressed, middle-aged man arrived. He questioned us about what we could do, and finally agreed to pay $1,000 for me, $900 for Harry and $700 for Eliza. When Eliza heard this, she became very upset[3] as she did not want to leave her children. But sadly she had no choice and as far as I know[4] she never heard of them again, though she talked about them day and night.

1 be taken 變成；得（病等）
2 weaken [ˋwikən] (v.) 變衰弱
3 upset [ʌpˋsɛt] (a.) 苦惱的
4 as far as I know 就我目前所知

Chapter 5

Ford and Tibeats

We were taken to the steamboat *Rodolph* and we traveled up the Mississippi River. Our master's name was William Ford, and he lived at Great Pine Woods on the banks of the Red River, in the middle of Louisiana. He was a very religious[1] man. Perhaps it seems strange that a man holding slaves could be religious, but it was the nature of the society which surrounded[2] him which blinded him to[3] the injustice[4] of slavery. However, he was a good master and his slaves were lucky to have him as a master.

We left the steamboat two days later at Alexandria, and drove eighteen miles towards Great Pine Woods in wagons. We had to walk the last twelve miles on foot.

Ford had a big house, for at that time he was a rich man, with various lumber[5] businesses. We were told to go to our cabin[6] and we were soon sleeping on the cabin floor. As I fell asleep I thought how impossible it would be to escape through these big forests.

1 religious [rɪˋlɪdʒəs] (a.) 宗教的；虔誠的
2 surround [səˋraʊnd] (v.) 圍繞
3 blind sb to sth 蒙蔽某人使得無法看到某事
4 injustice [ɪnˋdʒʌstɪs] (n.) 非正義；不公不義
5 lumber [ˋlʌmbɚ] (n.) 木材
6 cabin [ˋkæbɪn] (n.) 小屋

21 I was awakened next morning by Master Ford calling for his house slave, Rose, to go and dress his children. Another female slave, Sally, went to the field to milk the cows[7] while the young kitchen slave, John, went to cook the food.

Harry and I walked around the yard, looking at our new home. Later we met Rose's husband, Walton. Ford told Harry and I to go with Walton to pile[8] wood and chop logs[9], and we continued doing that work for the rest of the summer.

On Sundays, Ford gathered all his slaves together near his house, and read and talked about the Bible[10].

In the autumn, I worked around the Ford house. I also helped a visiting carpenter fix the ceiling in one of the rooms. His name was John M. Tibeats, a small, bad-tempered[11], ignorant[12] man who was the complete opposite[13] of Master Ford.

Unfortunately, in the winter of 1842 William Ford started having financial problems because of his brother, for whom he had given security[14]. Ford was heavily in debt to[15] Tibeats for buildings built on the cotton plantation and had to sell some of his slaves. I was sold to Tibeats, because of my skills as a carpenter.

7 milk the cow 擠牛奶
8 pile [paɪl] (v.) 堆積
9 log [lɔg] (n.) 原木
10 the Bible《聖經》
11 bad-tempered [ˋbædˋtɛmpɚd] (a.) 脾氣不好的
12 ignorant [ˋɪgnərənt] (a.) 沒有受教育的
13 opposite [ˋɑpəzɪt] (n.) 對立面；對立物
14 give security 作保人
15 in debt to sb 欠某人的債

22 As my value was more than his debt, Ford took out a chattel[1] mortgage[2] of $400, and as will be seen later in my story, I am indebted[3] for my life to that mortgage.

I went first with Tibeats to Ford's plantation twenty-seven miles away to complete unfinished buildings. I met Eliza, who worked there now. She had become weak and thin, and still missed her children terribly.

I worked from early morning until late at night, and Tibeats was never satisfied. While working on one of the buildings, I did something punishable by death in that state.

Tibeats had ordered me to get up early one morning and get a box of different nails from Ford's plantation overseer[4], Chapin. Chapin was a kind man and when I met with Chapin, he told me that if Tibeats wanted a different size of nail, he could bring them later, but for the moment I should continue with the nails I had. Chapin then rode off to check on the slaves working in the fields. I went to the building and started my work.

As the sun came up, Tibeats appeared. He examined my work.

"Didn't I tell you last night to get different nails from Chapin?" he asked.

1 chattel [ˋtʃætl̩] (n.) 動產
2 mortgage [ˋmɔrgɪdʒ] (n.) 抵押
3 indebted [ɪnˋdɛtɪd] (a.) 受惠的
4 overseer [ˋovɚˌsiɚ] (n.) 監督者；工頭

23 "Yes, master, and I did. The overseer said he could get another size for you later. He is in the fields now."

Tibeats looked at them, then came towards me in great anger. "Damn you![1] I thought you had a brain!" he shouted.

"I did what you told me to do, master. The overseer said . . ."

But Tibeats ran to the house and took one of Chapin's whips[2]. At first I was afraid, but my fear soon changed to anger. I decided that I didn't want to be whipped, whatever the result[3].

He walked up to me and ordered me to strip[4].

"Mr Tibeats," I said, looking him straight in the face, "I will not."

He jumped towards me, holding me by the throat with one hand, and raising the whip in the other. But before he could hit me, I reached down to his ankle and pushed him so that he fell over on the ground.

I took hold of one leg and held it to my chest, so that only his head and shoulders touched the ground, and I put my foot on his neck. He was completely in my power.

He struggled, and shouted that he wanted to kill me, but I took the whip from his hand, and hit him many times with the handle[5]. Chapin heard Tibeats's screams[6] and he rode in from the fields, so I kicked Tibeats away. He stood up and we stared[7] at each other in silence.

24 "What's the matter?" asked Chapin when he saw us.

"Master Tibeats wants to whip me for not using the different nails," I replied.

"I'm overseer here," Chapin began. "I told Platt to use them, and that I could get different ones later. It is not his fault. When I finish in the fields I will get the others, Mr Tibeats. Do you understand?"

Tibeats didn't answer, but he walked off to the house angrily shaking his fists[8]. He was followed by Chapin, and a heated[9] discussion[10] followed.

I stayed where I was, and soon after Tibeats came out and rode off on his horse. Chapin came over to me, and told me not to go anywhere. He said my master, Mr Tibeats, was a bad man, and that there might be trouble soon.

I spent the next hour in total misery[11] and fear, realizing the seriousness of what I had done. I, a poor black slave, had assaulted[12] a *white* man, who was also my master.

Tibeats returned with two other men. They got off their horses carrying two long whips and a length of rope.

"Cross your hands," ordered Tibeats.

1 damn you〔罵人的話〕去你的
2 whip [hwɪp] (n.) 鞭子 (v.) 鞭打
3 result [rɪˋzʌlt] (n.) 結果
4 strip [strɪp] (v.) 脫掉衣服
5 handle [ˋhændḷ] (n.) 把手
6 scream [skrim] (n.) 尖叫聲
7 stare [stɛr] (v.) 盯；凝視
8 fist [fɪst] (n.) 拳頭
9 heated [ˋhitɪd] (a.) 激烈的
10 discussion [dɪˋskʌʃən] (n.) 討論
11 misery [ˋmɪzərɪ] (n.) 痛苦；不幸
12 assault [əˋsɔlt] (v.) 攻擊；襲擊

25 "You don't need to tie me, master. I am ready to go with you," I replied.

But the three men tied my arms and legs so that I could not move. Then Tibeats made a noose[1] and put it around my neck. I could see Chapin by the door of his house. I lost hope, and felt that now I was definitely[2] going to die.

"Now, then," said one of Tibeats's friends, "where shall we hang[3] the slave?"

"That peach tree," suggested the other.

They dragged[4] me towards it, however Chapin came walking towards us with a pistol[5] in each hand. "Gentlemen, I have a few words to say, so listen," he said. "Whoever moves that slave one inch more is a dead man. In the first place[6], he does not deserve[7] this treatment. I never knew a more faithful[8] man than Platt. You, Tibeats, are in the wrong[9] yourself. You are a bad man, and really deserved the beating you got this morning. Next, I am overseer and master here. My duty is to protect William Ford's interests[10]. He holds a mortgage of $400 on Platt. If you hang him, he loses the money. Until that money has been paid, you have no right to kill Platt. You have no right to anyway. There is a law for the slave as well as for the white man. You are no better than a murderer[11]."

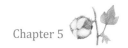

26 He turned to the other two, who were overseers on nearby plantations: "You two—get out of here!"

Without another word, they got on their horses and rode away.

Tibeats, clearly afraid of Chapin, left quietly like a coward[12], and rode after his friends.

Chapin then called another slave—Lawson. "Lawson," said Chapin, "get the fast brown mule[13] and go as quickly as possible to Pine Woods and tell your master, Ford, to come here at once. Tell him they are trying to murder Platt. Now, hurry!"

Chapin

- How does Chapin save Platt (Solomon) here? Go back to page 36.

1 noose [nus] (n.) 套索
2 definitely [ˋdɛfənɪtlɪ] (adv.) 明確地；清楚地
3 hang [hæŋ] (v.) 吊死（三態：hang; hanged; hanged）
4 drag [dræg] (v.) 拖
5 pistol [ˋpɪstl̩] (n.) 手槍

6 in the first place 首先
7 deserve [dɪˋzɝv] (v.) 應受；該得
8 faithful [ˋfeθfəl] (a.) 忠實的
9 in the wrong 錯誤；不應該
10 interest [ˋɪntərɪst] (n.) 利益
11 murderer [ˋmɝdərɚ] (n.) 謀殺犯
12 coward [ˋkauɚd] (n.) 懦夫；膽怯者
13 mule [mjul] (n.) 騾

Chapter 6

The hot sun

27 I stood in the baking[1] sun the whole day, in pain from the tight ropes and being completely unable to move, while Chapin stayed near his house, watching me. He obviously[2] thought Tibeats wanted to come back with more helpers. I presumed[3] he wanted Ford to see me exactly as Tibeats had left me.

At sunset Ford arrived. Chapin met him, and after a short conversation, he walked over to me.

"Poor Platt, you are in a bad state," was all that he said to me.

"Thank God, Master Ford, that you have come at last," I replied.

He cut the ropes from my arms and legs and took the noose off my neck. I tried to walk, but fell to the ground.

Ford returned to the house, and as he reached it, Tibeats and his two friends arrived on their horses. A long discussion followed, and the three left again, clearly unhappy with the outcome[4].

1 baking [ˋbekɪŋ] (a.) 灼熱的
2 obviously [ˋɑbvɪəslɪ] (adv.) 顯然地
3 presume [prɪˋzum] (v.) 設想；認為
4 outcome [ˋaʊtˏkʌm] (n.) 後果；結局

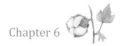

28 I crawled[5] into the cabin and lay down. I was in great misery, and the smallest movement was painful. Soon the other slaves came back from the fields. Eliza and Mary fried me some maize[6] and made coffee.

They asked what had happened. I explained and Lawson talked about his trip to Pine Woods. They were full of sympathy[7], saying what a cruel man Tibeats was, and hoping that Master Ford could take me back again.

Then Chapin appeared at the cabin door. "Platt," he said, "you'll sleep on the floor in the house tonight." He thought Tibeats might come back in the morning, intending to[8] kill me.

With the fear of danger and the pain in my body, I slept little that night.

Next morning, I got up with difficulty, and after breakfast I went out to start work. I felt the misery of slavery on me then. Working long hours day after day, listening to the insults[9] of others, sleeping on the hard ground, eating poor food, and worst of all[10], working for a horrible man whom I must always fear.

I longed for[11] liberty, thinking of the thousands of miles that lay between me and the freedom of the north.

5 crawl [krɔl] (v.) 爬行
6 maize [mez] (n.) 玉蜀黍

7 sympathy [ˋsɪmpəθɪ] (n.) 同情
8 intend to 打算
9 insult [ˋɪnsʌlt] (n.) 羞辱
10 worst of all 最慘的是
11 long for . . . 渴望……

29

Ford went back to Pine Woods later that day. I constantly[1] feared Tibeats and what he could do to me at any moment. But he seemed to keep his distance, only coming to check my work when necessary.

During the week, the building I was working on was completed. Tibeats told me that he had hired[2] me to Peter Tanner, Mistress[3] Ford's brother, who had a plantation on the other side of the river.

I was to work under another carpenter called Myers. I was very pleased to be free of Tibeats for a while. On arrival, I found that everyone already knew about me, because of my good work for Ford and for beating Tibeats. Tanner warned me, however, to be on good behavior.

I then worked under Myers for a month to his and my own satisfaction.

Work

- Why is respect and collaboration[4] in the work place so important? Discuss in groups.

1 constantly [ˋkɑnstəntlɪ] (adv.) 時常地
2 hire [haɪr] (v.) 租借
3 mistress [ˋmɪstrɪs] (n.) 女主人
4 collaboration [kə͵læbəˋreʃən] (n.) 合作

Chapter 7

My escape

30 I was sent back to Ford's plantation where Tibeats was building a cotton press[1]. As this was some distance from the great house, I usually worked alone with him. I remembered what Chapin had said about Tibeats trying to do something to me, and felt nervous most of the time.

On the third morning, when Chapin was away in Cheneyville, Tibeats had one of his attacks[2] of bad temper.

I was planing[3] a plank[4], while he stood by the workbench[5].

"You're not planing that down enough," he said.

"It's level[6] with the line," I replied.

"You're a liar," he shouted.

"Oh well, master," I said mildly[7], "I'll plane it down more if you want me to."

I did so but he shouted that I had now planed it too much. He started insulting me. I stood in silence and fear, not knowing what to do. He grew more and more violent[8] and finally picked up a hatchet[9] and ran towards me saying he wanted to cut my head open.

1 cotton press 榨棉機
2 attack [ə`tæk] (n.) 攻擊
3 plane [plen] (v.) 刨平
4 plank [plæŋk] (n.) 木板條；厚板

31 It was a moment of life or death. I jumped on him, pulled the hatchet from his hand and threw it away. Mad with anger, he took a long, thick piece of wood and rushed towards me. I pushed him down to the ground, got the wood from him and threw that away, too.

However, he stood and ran for an axe[10] which was lying on the ground. I jumped onto his back, so that he couldn't get it. Something inside me said I should kill him, but I knew I was sure to be executed[11] for murder. On the other hand, if he lived, he was sure to kill me. The only thing to do was run away.

I pushed Tibeats onto the ground, jumped over a wall and hurried across the plantation, passing the cotton field. There I climbed up onto the high wall and looked back. I saw Tibeats getting on his horse and galloping[12] away.

What was going to happen to me now? Who could help me? Where should I go? A little later I saw Tibeats and two others on horses riding in my direction, followed by eight to ten dogs. I knew that they were the special kind of dog used for hunting slaves and that, from their savage[13] cries, they were not far behind me.

5 workbench [ˋwɝk͵bɛntʃ] (n.) 工作臺
6 level [ˋlɛvl̩] (a.) 同高度的（後接 with）
7 mildly [ˋmaɪldlɪ] (adv.) 和善地
8 violent [ˋvaɪələnt] (a.) 兇暴的
9 hatchet [ˋhætʃɪt] (n.)（劈木頭用的）短柄小斧
10 axe [æks] (n.)（砍伐樹木用的）斧頭
11 execute [ˋɛksɪ͵kjut] (v.) 處死
12 gallop [ˋgæləp] (n.) 騎馬疾馳
13 savage [ˋsævɪdʒ] (a.) 兇猛的

32 I ran towards the swamp[1]. Fear gave me strength. I could hear the dogs getting closer. I was gasping[2] for breath as I ran into a watery area.

I knew that the water might lose my scent[3] and confuse the dogs. Fortunately, I soon came to a wide river, and I swam across it. My scent was sure to be lost, leaving the dogs nothing to follow.

I was now in the main swamp. It was filled with different kinds of tall trees and extended[4] for miles with only bears, wild cats and reptiles[5] living there. I had to be very careful where I stepped and put my hands because it was full of poisonous[6] snakes, and alligators lying in the water.

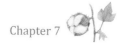

33 At about two o'clock in the afternoon I heard the last of the dogs. I now worried more about the snakes and alligators.

As I walked on slowly through the swamp. I knew I was nearer to human habitation[7] now and I began to get worried. Without a pass[8], any white man was free to arrest me and take me prisoner[9] until my master came to claim[10] me. I didn't know which I should fear most—dogs, alligators or men!

After the moon had risen, I decided on a different plan. I started traveling in a northwest direction instead of south. I was moving towards the pine woods near William Ford's house. I was sure to be safer there.

1 swamp [swɑmp] (n.) 沼澤
2 gasp [gæsp] (v.) 上氣不接下氣
3 scent [sɛnt] (n.) 氣味
4 extend [ɪk`stɛnd] (v.) 綿延
5 reptile [`rɛptaɪl] (n.) 爬蟲類動物
6 poisonous [`pɔɪzn̩əs] (a.) 有毒的
7 habitation [ˏhæbə`teʃən] (n.) 住處
8 pass [pæs] (n.) 通行證
9 prisoner [`prɪzn̩ɚ] (n.) 囚犯
10 claim [klem] (v.) 認領

34

My clothes were torn[1], my hands, face and body were covered in cuts[2] from the trees. I had lost one shoe. I was covered with mud and dirt. Eventually I found myself on dry land and knew I was somewhere near the Great Pine Woods.

At daybreak[3], I came to a clearing[4] where a master and his slave were hunting wild pigs. Knowing that the white man could take me prisoner, I chose go up to him directly: with a fierce[5] expression[6] on my face. I walked straight up to the white man and looked him in the eye.

"Where does William Ford live?" I asked roughly[7].

"Six miles from here," he answered. "Go to those two tall pine trees. You will find the Texas road. Turn to the left and it will lead you to William Ford's."

I followed his instructions[8] and by eight o'clock I reached Master Ford's house. I found Ford and told him the whole story. He listened, and spoke to me sympathetically[9].

I was given food, then I went to the cabin where I slept, feeling great relief[10].

1 tear [tɛr] (v.) 扯破
（三態：tear; tore; torn）
2 cut [kʌt] (n.) 傷口
3 daybreak [ˋde͵brek] (n.) 黎明；破曉
4 clearing [ˋklɪrɪŋ] (n.) 林中的空地
5 fierce [fɪrs] (a.) 兇狠的
6 expression [ɪkˋsprɛʃən] (n.) 表情
7 roughly [ˋrʌflɪ] (adv.) 粗暴地
8 instructions [ɪnˋstrʌkʃənz] (n.)〔複〕指示
9 sympathetically [͵sɪmpəˋθɛtɪklɪ] (adv.) 同情地
10 relief [rɪˋlif] (n.) 緩和；減輕
11 repay [rɪˋpe] (v.) 報答
12 weed [wid] (n.) 雜草
13 not in a fit state 無能力
14 assure [əˋʃur] (v.) 確保
15 alongside [əˋlɔŋˋsaɪd] (prep.) 在……旁
16 adventure [ədˋvɛntʃɚ] (n.) 冒險

Chapter 8

Epps

35 The next afternoon, I went to Mistress Ford's garden. It was full of beautiful flowers and fruit. I wished to repay[11] the Fords in some way, so I started to pull out the weeds[12] in the garden. Mistress Ford came out and praised me, but said that I was not in a fit state[13] to work. I assured[14] her that the work was easy and that it was a pleasure to work for such a good mistress. And so for the next three days I cleared the weeds in her garden.

On the fourth morning, Master Ford ordered me to go with him to the swamp. On the way, we met Tibeats. He did not speak to me, but rode alongside[15] Ford talking.

Ford told him about my adventures[16], and Tibeats spoke about the hunt and said he thought I had died in the swamp. Ford told Tibeats that he had treated me very badly, and that it was all his fault.

36 "It is clear, Mr Tibeats, that you and Platt cannot live together. You dislike him and want to kill him. He knows that, and will run away. You must either sell him, or hire him out to someone else. Unless you do, I'll take him away from you."

I went back to the plantation, and the next morning when I met Tibeats he told me he had sold me to a man called Edwin Epps.

We went straight to Epps's plantation. Epps examined me and asked me the usual questions a buyer asks a slave. I felt greatly relieved[1] that I was no longer the property of Tibeats.

I was sure that this new master was a change for the better.

Edwin Epps was over six feet tall, a big man, with light hair, blue eyes, high cheek bones and a very large nose. He spoke in an uneducated[2] way and his manners[3] were disgusting. He also drank a lot. When drunk[4], he danced noisily with his slaves, or whipped them; when sober[5], he was quiet and cunning, whipping his slaves in unusual and unexpected ways.

At this time he had leased[6] a plantation called Huff Power near a bayou[7] from his wife's uncle, where he grew cotton.

At Master Epps's plantation, ploughing[8], planting and picking cotton, gathering corn and pulling up the old plants occupied[9] most of the slaves' time throughout the year.

37 In the cotton-picking season all slaves were expected to pick at least eighty-five kilos of cotton a day, although some could pick more. Those who didn't pick the correct amount of cotton were whipped.

We worked each day from dawn until dusk[10], with only fifteen minutes' break. When the driver said stop, the cotton was weighed[11].

The slave always approaches[12] the scales[13] in fear. If he has not picked enough, he knows he will suffer[14], and if he has picked more, he will have to pick that amount the next day, too. Either way he loses!

After the weighing and whipping, the slaves carry their basket to the cotton house. Then there are other jobs to do—feeding the mules and pigs, cutting wood—all done by candlelight.

Finally, we reached our cabins, exhausted[15], and had to make a fire, and cook supper and lunch for the next day. All we had was corn and bacon, which were given out each Sunday morning. By the time the food was ready, it was usually midnight.

1 relieved [rɪˋlivd] (a.) 放心的
2 uneducated [ʌnˋɛdʒʊˏketɪd] (a.) 未受教育的
3 manner [ˋmænɚ] (n.) 舉止態度
4 drunk [drʌŋk] (a.) 喝醉酒的
5 sober [ˋsobɚ] (a.) 沒喝醉的
6 lease [lis] (v.) 出租（土地等）
7 bayou [ˋbaɪu] (n.) 海灣
8 plough [plaʊ] (v.) 犁地；耕地
9 occupy [ˋɑkjəˏpaɪ] (v.) 佔據
10 dusk [dʌsk] (n.) 黃昏
11 weigh [we] (v.) 稱……的重量
12 approach [əˋprotʃ] (v.) 接近
13 scale [skel] (n.) 秤
14 suffer [ˋsʌfɚ] (v.) 受苦
15 exhausted [ɪgˋzɔstɪd] (a.) 精疲力竭的

38 Slaves sleep in constant[1] fear that they will wake up late next morning, which means twenty lashes[2] with the whip. During my time with Epps, I slept on a plank 30 cm wide, with a branch[3] for a pillow and a rough blanket for my bedding.

An hour before daylight a horn is blown, and the slaves get up. They fill a gourd[4] with water, and another with their lunch of cold bacon and corn cake and hurry to the field again. Any slave found in the cabin after daybreak will be beaten.

Cotton picking lasts from the end of August until January. Then the harvesting[5] of corn starts. Corn is not an important crop there, and is used mainly for feeding the pigs and the slaves. The leaves are stripped in August to provide food for the animals, and the rest is often left to be picked in February.

Slaves

- Write a list of all the different things the slaves on Epps's plantation had to do each day.
- Is Platt's new master a change for the better? Discuss with a partner.

1 constant [ˋkɑnstənt] (a.) 接連不斷的
2 lash [læʃ] (n.) 鞭打
3 branch [bræntʃ] (n.) 樹枝
4 gourd [gord] (n.) 葫蘆
5 harvesting [ˋhɑrvɪstɪŋ] (n.) 收割

Chapter 9

The whipping and the dancing

39 When I first arrived at Master Epps's I got a fever[1] and became weak and thin. I had to keep working, but found it difficult to work quickly, and so got whipped by the driver[2]. Finally, in September, I was unable to leave the cabin. I received no medicine or attention from my master or mistress. Only the old cook sometimes visited me and made me corn coffee or boiled me some bacon.

When the others said I was dying, Epps finally called the doctor. This was only because he didn't want to lose an animal worth $1,000.

The doctor said it was due to the climate, and said I should eat no meat and little else. After a few weeks of this diet, I was partly better, and so Epps ordered me out to the cotton field.

40 I had no experience of picking cotton, and found it very difficult. At the end of the day I had only forty kilos—only half the correct daily amount. Epps excused[3] me as I was new to the work. However, I was unable to increase this quantity despite[4] practice and whipping.

Epps said I was a disgrace[5] and took me out of the cotton field. I then cut and moved wood, took cotton to be weighed and did other necessary jobs.

It was unusual for a day to pass without a whipping. This happened after the cotton was weighed. The slave to be punished was made to strip and lie face downwards on the ground to receive the lashes. Twenty-five was the basic number of lashes for minor[6] offenses[7] such as a dry leaf found in your sack of cotton; one hundred were given to slaves seen not working; two hundred to those found fighting; five hundred, plus the bites of the dogs, to those who ran away.

On Epps's plantation, the crack[8] of the whip and the screams of the slaves could be heard from dark until bedtime throughout the cotton-picking season.

1 fever [ˋfivɚ] (n.) 發燒
2 driver [ˋdraɪvɚ] (n.) 驅趕者；工頭
3 excuse [ɪkˋskjuz] (v.) 原諒
4 despite [dɪˋspaɪt] (prep.) 儘管
5 disgrace [dɪsˋgres] (n.) 丟臉
6 minor [ˋmaɪnɚ] (a.) 微小的；不重要的
7 offense [əˋfɛns] (n.) 違反規定
8 crack [kræk] (n.) 爆裂聲

41 Whenever he visited Holmesville, Epps came home drunk. After breaking all the plates and chairs in his house, he either walked around the yard whipping anyone he saw, or demanded music and dancing.

As Tibeats had told him I could play the violin, I was frequently called to play. When Epps wanted dancing, everyone had to gather in the large room of the house, and no matter how[1] tired after work the slaves were, they had to dance.

"Dance, you damned slaves, dance," Epps shouted.

And there was no rest. The whip was ready for anyone who dared[2] to stop dancing to catch their breath[3]. This went on almost until morning, but we all had to be in the fields at daybreak the next day. And the whippings were just the same if anyone had less cotton than expected the evening after. If anything[4], his temper[5] was worse after those night dances than usual.

1 no matter how 不管怎樣
2 dare [dɛr] (v.) 敢；竟敢
3 catch one's breath 喘氣
4 if anything 如果有區別的話
5 temper [ˋtɛmpɚ] (n.) 脾氣

Chapter 10
Christmas

Epps remained on Huff Power for two years. By then he'd earned enough money to buy a plantation of his own on the other bank of the bayou. He moved there in 1845, taking with him nine slaves, including myself, and for eight years they were my companions[1] there.

In the first year at Epps's new plantation, in 1845, insects destroyed the cotton crop[2] throughout the region. The slaves thus had no work to do and we were taken to cut sugar cane[3] on the Gulf of Mexico. When the work was finished, we were taken home. However, for the next three years Epps hired me out in the cane-cutting season at $1 a day, which was good money for him.

The following summer, I found a way of improving[4] my diet. We slaves were given weekly rations[5] of smoked bacon and corn, however in summer the meat was often full of maggots[6], and inedible[7].

1 companion [kəm`pænjən] (n.) 同伴
2 crop [krɑp] (n.) 收成
3 sugar cane 甘蔗
4 improve [ɪm`pruv] (v.) 改善

43 Some slaves went out into the bayou at night to hunt raccoon[8] or other wild animals for extra meat. But going hunting after a day's work was hard. As my cabin was close to the bayou, I invented a successful fish trap[9] and from then on I and my friends always had fresh fish.

The only break a slave has from work is at Christmas. Epps allowed us three days. It is a time of feasting[10] and pleasure, when everyone forgets their own problems. The slaves have a little limited liberty and they enjoy it completely.

Changing place every year, the planters[11] give a "Christmas supper" for their own slaves and those from neighboring plantations. Around four hundred attend[12]. They get dressed in their best clothes. The table is set up outside and we eat chicken, duck, turkey, pork with vegetables. There are also biscuits with peach jam, pies and other sweets. The men slaves sit on one side and women on the other side of the long table, and there is much joking and laughter as they eat.

5 ration [ˋræʃən] (n.) 配給量
6 maggot [ˋmægət] (n.) 蛆
7 inedible [ɪnˋɛdəbl̩] (a.) 不適合食用的
8 raccoon [ræˋkun] (n.) 浣熊
9 trap [træp] (n.) 捕捉器
10 feasting [ˋfistɪŋ] (n.) 盛宴款待
11 planter [ˋplæntɚ] (n.) 大農場主
12 attend [əˋtɛnd] (v.) 出席；參加

44

After the meal comes the Christmas dance. My job was to play the violin. And indeed, if it had not been for my beloved[1] violin, I don't know how I could have survived[2] my years as a slave. It meant that I could play at parties in planters' houses and so earn some money, and it was also my friend in times of happiness and sadness. And Christmas was always special, because I could help my fellow slaves to enjoy dancing in the starlight[3].

After Christmas Day, slaves are given passes and allowed to go where they want within a limited distance. This freedom from work and fear of the whip brings an enormous[4] change in the appearance and behavior of the slaves. They visit old friends and travel around the area; it is also the time when most slave marriages take place, something which only requires[5] the agreement[6] of both slave owners.

Christmas

- Compare[7] your Christmas to a slave's Christmas.

1 beloved [bɪˋlʌvɪd] (a.) 心愛的
2 survive [sɚˋvaɪv] (v.) 活下來
3 starlight [ˋstɑrˏlaɪt] (n.) 星光
4 enormous [ɪˋnɔrməs] (a.) 巨大的
5 require [rɪˋkwaɪr] (v.) 需要
6 agreement [əˋgrimənt] (n.) 同意
7 compare [kəmˋpɛr] (v.) 比較
8 apart from 除……外
9 heartlessness [ˋhɑrtlɪsnɪs] (n.) 冷酷；無情
10 brutality [bruˋtælətɪ] (n.) 殘忍
11 share [ʃɛr] (n.) 份兒
12 force [fors] (v.) 迫使

Chapter 11

The letter

45 Apart from[8] the cane-cutting seasons, I worked on Epps's plantation all the time. He was a small planter, and didn't have an overseer like Chapin at Master Ford's. The overseer rides out to the field on a horse, with a whip, pistols and knife, and several dogs. The qualifications for an overseer are heartlessness[9], brutality[10] and cruelty. It is his business to produce large crops, and it is not important what suffering it costs.

Under the overseer there are one or more drivers. They are black slaves who, as well as doing their share[11] of the work, are also forced[12] to whip the gangs they control. They wear a whip around their neck and if they do not use them, they are whipped themselves.

When Epps moved to the new plantation, I was made driver, and Epps did the overseer's work.

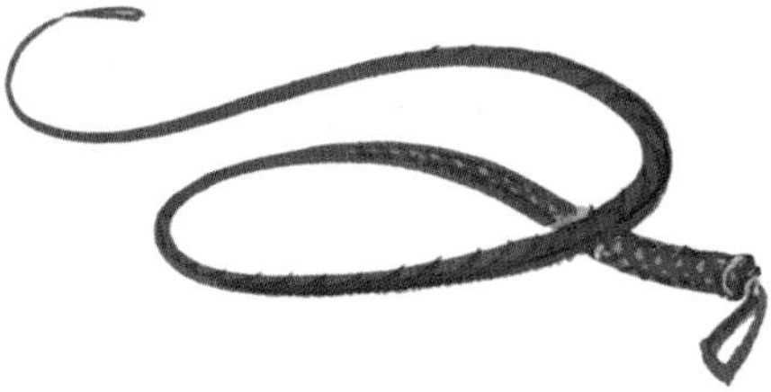

46

If Epps was present[1], I didn't dare to be gentle. However, even when Epps was not with us, he watched what was happening from a hidden[2] place. If someone didn't work hard all the time, Epps whipped them, and also whipped me for allowing it. When he saw me use the whip often, he praised me.

But, during my eight years as a driver, I learnt to use the whip so precisely, that I could make the whip come very close to the back without touching it. My friends had learned to squirm[3] and scream in pain to make Epps believe that they were being hit.

Epps once asked me if I could read and write. When I told him I could, he said that if he ever saw me with a book or pen and ink, he would give me one hundred lashes.

"I buy slaves to work, not to educate," he said.

My main aim[4] always was to find a way of getting a letter to some of my friends or family. This was almost impossible. I couldn't get pen, ink or paper and no slave could leave the plantation without a pass, and a postmaster[5] never sent a letter for a slave without written instructions from the slave's owner. It took me nine years, to find a chance.

1 present [ˋprɛzənt] (a.) 在場的
2 hidden [ˋhɪdn̩] (a.) 隱藏的；隱祕的
3 squirm [skwɝm] (v.) 蠕動；扭動
4 aim [em] (n.) 目標
5 postmaster [ˋpost͵mæstɚ] (n.) 郵政局長
6 bark [bɑrk] (n.) 樹皮
7 communication [kə͵mjunəˋkeʃən] (n.) 交流；通訊
8 means [minz] (n.)〔單〕方法；工具

47 Epps was in New Orleans, selling cotton; the mistress sent me to Holmesville to buy several articles, including paper. I took one sheet of the paper and hid it under the board I slept on. I made ink by boiling maple tree bark[6], and a pen from a duck feather.

At night, I completed a long letter to an old friend at Sandy Hill explaining my situation and asking his help in getting my freedom. I kept this letter for a long time, trying to find a way of getting it safely to a post office.

Communication[7]

- How do you communicate with people?
- How often do you use this means[8] of communication?

Once a man called Armsby came looking for work as an overseer. He stayed with Epps for several days. I found ways of talking to him, and when he said that he often visited Marksville, a town eighteen miles away, I decided that he might send my letter.

48 One night I went to where Armsby was sleeping, and asked for his help. I begged him not to tell Epps if he could not post the letter. He said he could both post it and keep it a secret.

Two days later, however, I saw Armsby talking with Epps at length[1], and that night Epps came to my cabin with a whip in his hand.

"Well, boy," he said. "It seems I've got a clever slave who writes letters and tries to ask someone to send them. I wonder who he is?"

"I don't know anything about it, Master Epps." I replied.

"Didn't you speak to Armsby about it?" he asked.

"Certainly not," I replied. "I never spoke more than three words to him."

"Armsby says you woke him up," said Epps, "and asked him to take a letter to Marksville."

"It's not true, master," I answered. "How could I write a letter without ink or paper? There's nobody I want to write to because I have no living[2] friends. Armsby is a lying[3], drunken[4] man, they say, and nobody believes him. I can see his plan clearly. He wants to be your overseer, and he thinks if he makes up[5] a story like this, then you'll hire him to watch us."

"Well, Platt, I believe you're telling the truth. Armsby must think I'm stupid, coming here with stories like that."

Betrayal[6]

- Have you ever been betrayed[7] by someone you thought you could trust?
- How did you feel?
- What were the consequences of this betrayal for you? Tell a friend.

49

Epps left the cabin. It broke my heart but I immediately burnt my letter. I didn't want to risk anything.

Armsby was thrown off[8] Epps's plantation the next day, much to my relief.

I didn't know how I might be saved. I felt I was growing old and that after a few more years of hard work and misery, my destiny[9] was to die and be forgotten. Only the hope of rescue gave me any comfort, but that hope was now very small. I prepared myself to live in darkness to the end of my life.

1 at length 經過一段長時間之後；終於
2 living [ˋlɪvɪŋ] (a.) 活著的
3 lying [ˋlaɪɪŋ] (a.) 說謊的
4 drunken [ˋdrʌŋkən] (a.) 常酗酒的
5 make up 編造
6 betrayal [bɪˋtreəl] (n.) 背叛
7 betray [bɪˋtre] (v.) 背叛；洩漏
8 throw off 擺脫某人
9 destiny [ˋdɛstənɪ] (n.) 命運

Chapter 12

Bass

50 In June 1852, Epps ordered me to help a carpenter called Mr Avery build a house for him. Among Avery's men was one called Bass who helped get me my freedom.

Bass was a bachelor[1] of about forty-five, and lived in Marksville, visiting his home once a fortnight. He was a kind and liberal[2] man, always ready to discuss any topic from politics[3] to religion[4].

One day, Bass and Epps got into an argument about slavery. I listened with great interest.

"It's all wrong, Epps," said Bass. "I wouldn't own a slave if I were a millionaire[5]. What right do you have to own black slaves?"

"What right!" said Epps, laughing. "Why, I bought them!"

"Of course you did. The law says you can do that, but the law is wrong," stated Bass. "Now, what is the difference between a white man and a black one?"

1 bachelor [ˋbætʃələ˞] (n.) 單身漢
2 liberal [ˋlɪbərəl] (a.) 心胸寬闊的
3 politics [ˋpɑlətɪks] (n.) 政治
4 religion [rɪˋlɪdʒən] (n.) 宗教
5 millionaire [͵mɪljənˋɛr] (n.) 百萬富翁

51 "All the difference in the world[1]," replied Epps. "You might as well[2] ask what the difference is between a white man and a monkey!"

"But Epps," continued Bass, "are all men created free and equal as the Declaration of Independence says they are?"

"Yes," responded[3] Epps, "but all *men*—not slaves and monkeys."

All men

- Use the Internet to find some information about the Declaration of Independence.

"There are monkeys among white people, too," remarked[4] Bass coolly[5]. "These slaves are human beings. They're not allowed to know anything. You have books and papers, and can go where you please, but your slaves have no privileges[6]. You'd whip one you caught reading a book. This goes on generation[7] after generation. Slavery is evil and should be abolished."

52 Here Epps stood up and left, but there were similar conversations after this.

I decided Bass was the man I could tell about my situation. One day we were working alone together and so I took my chance[8].

"Master Bass, where do you come from?" I started.

"Why, Platt," he answered, "you wouldn't know even if I told you. But I was born in Canada."

"I've been there," I said. "I've been to Montreal, Kingston and Queenstown. And I've been in York State, too—in Buffalo, Rochester and Albany."

"Why are you here?" he asked. "Who are you?"

I told him it was a long story, and that Epps was sure to return soon. I asked him to meet me in that house again after midnight. He promised to keep everything I said secret.

We met as planned, and I told him my story. I begged him to write to my friends in the north to help me get my freedom back. He agreed to do so, but also reminded me of the danger of death he faced for informing about me. We then made a plan.

1 all the difference in the world 完完全全不一樣
2 might as well 不妨；倒不如
3 respond [rɪˋspɑnd] (v.) 回應
4 remark [rɪˋmɑrk] (v.) 議論；評論
5 coolly [ˋkulɪ] (adv.) 冷靜地
6 privilege [ˋprɪvḷɪdʒ] (n.) 特權
7 generation [ˏdʒɛnəˋreʃən] (n.) 世代
8 take one's chance 碰運氣；準備冒險

53 The next night we met again and he noted down the names and addresses of those I wanted him to write to, but then said: "It's many years since you left Saratoga. All these men may be dead or have moved. You said you got papers from the Customs House in New York. Probably there is a record[1] of them there, so I think it would be good to write to them, too."

I agreed, saying how grateful[2] I would be if he helped me gain[3] my freedom. He said that as an unmarried man with no family, he was happy to give all his attention to getting my liberty.

When Bass next returned from Marksville he told me he'd spent Sunday writing letters to the Customs House in New York, to Judge[4] Marvin, and to Mr Parker and Mr Perry jointly[5]. It was this last letter which led to my release.

From then on whenever he visited Marksville I was very excited, only to be disappointed when he returned with nothing.

Ten weeks passed, and the house was finished. The night before Bass's departure[6] I was in complete despair[7]. He said he was coming back the day before Christmas, and that he wanted to continue in his quest[8] for my freedom.

Bass kept his word[9], arriving on Christmas Eve. Epps took him to the great house where he stayed the night. Early in the morning, he came to my cabin.

1 record [ˋrɛkɚd] (n.) 記錄
2 grateful [ˋgretfəl] (a.) 感激的
3 gain [gen] (v.) 獲得
4 judge [dʒʌdʒ] (n.) 法官
5 jointly [ˋdʒɔɪntlɪ] (adv.) 連帶地
6 departure [dɪˋpɑrtʃɚ] (n.) 離開
7 despair [dɪˋspɛr] (n.) 絕望
8 quest [kwɛst] (n.) 尋求
9 keep one's word 遵守諾言

54

"No letter yet, Platt," he said.

The news was like a weight[1] on my heart.

"Oh, please write again, Master Bass," I cried. "I will give you the names of others I know."

"No," Bass replied. "The postmaster in Marksville will become suspicious[2]. But," continued Bass, "I have decided to go to Saratoga myself. I have some jobs to finish by March or April, and then I will have enough money to go there."

I could hardly believe his words.

"I must go now," he said. "Epps will soon get up and I mustn't be found here. But I will come again soon, and before that think of all the people you know in Saratoga and Sandy Hill. I'll write down their names, and will know who to visit when I go north. Cheer up[3]! I am with you[4]!"

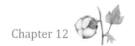

On January 3rd, 1853 we were out working. It was a cold morning, which is unusual for that region.

Epps came out *without* his whip—a very unusual event[5]—and one slave dared to say that he couldn't pick fast because his fingers were so cold. Epps swore[6] because he had no whip to beat him with, and rode off to get it.

While he was away, we noticed a carriage passing quickly towards the house, and later saw two men approaching us through the cotton field.

1 weight [wet] (n.)（精神的）壓力
2 suspicious [səˋspɪʃəs] (a.) 猜疑的
3 cheer up 振作起來
4 I am with you 我和你在一起
5 event [ɪˋvɛnt] (n.) 事件
6 swear [swɛr] (v.) 詛咒；罵髒話（三態：swear; swore; sworn）

Chapter 13

The letter home

55 Before continuing, I must go back and explain what happened after Bass had posted those three letters on August 15th, 1852.

The one addressed to Parker and Perry arrived in Saratoga in the early part of September. Parker and Perry forwarded[1] the letter to my wife Anne, who went immediately to get advice from Henry B. Northup in Sandy Hill.

He found there was a law from 1840 allowing the authorities of one state to get the release of one of its citizens[2] who had been kidnapped and kept as a slave in another state. To do this, two facts had to be proved[3]: first, that he was a free citizen and second that he was illegally held as a slave.

The documents were collected and Henry B. Northup was appointed[4] to deal with[5] everything.

Northup left on December 14th. He went to Washington, where he got further legal documents to give to the authorities in Louisiana. He then traveled south to Marksville, arriving at nine o'clock on the morning of January 1st, 1853. He presented the documents to a lawyer called John P. Waddill at the court[6] in Marksville.

56 The letter from Bass, however, was written in my real name—Solomon Northup. I was not known by that name as a slave but as Platt, so the task[7] of finding me seemed impossible.

As it was Sunday, they decided to leave to go back home the following day, and Northup spent time with Waddill. They talked about the different attitude[8] to slavery in the north.

Northup asked Waddill if he knew anyone in Marksville who talked against slavery, and Waddill replied that the only one was Bass. He then had a thought, and looked at the letter sent to Saratoga again.

"But, this is Bass's handwriting[9]!" Waddill shouted. "Bass is the man who can tell us about Solomon Northup."

They found Bass waiting for a boat by the river. He was preparing to leave for two weeks. They found him just in time[10] before he got on the boat!

"Mr Bass," said Northup. "I have come from New York. I am looking for the person who wrote a letter about Solomon Northup. If you know him, please tell me where I can find him. I assure you I will not give any information about you to anyone."

1 forward [ˋfɔrwɚd] (v.) 轉交
2 citizen [ˋsɪtəzn̩] (n.) 公民
3 prove [pruv] (v.) 證明
4 appoint [əˋpɔɪnt] (v.) 委任
5 deal with 處理
6 court [kort] (n.) 法院
7 task [tæsk] (n.) 任務
8 attitude [ˋætətjud] (n.) 態度
9 handwriting [ˋhænd͵raɪtɪŋ] (n.) 筆跡
10 just in time 及時

57 "I wrote that letter," Bass replied. "If you've come to rescue Solomon Northup, I'm glad to see you. He is the slave of Edwin Epps, a planter near Holmesville. They call him Platt."

Bass then explained the quickest route[1] to get there.

Northup still had to complete the necessary documents. Things suddenly became urgent when Waddill heard that Bass had left town and that a rumor[2] was circulating[3] that the stranger at the hotel (Northup) and Waddill were trying to free one of Epps's slaves.

Waddill was worried that the news might travel quickly to Epps, so they got the judge to sign[4] the documents after midnight, and the carriage with the sheriff[5] and Mr Northup left immediately that night.

They decided that the sheriff was going to ask me some personal questions before I spoke to Northup. If I answered the questions correctly, then the evidence was to be believed completely.

1 route [rut] (n.) 路線
2 rumor [ˋrumɚ] (n.) 謠言；傳聞
3 circulate [ˋsɝkjə͵let] (v.) 流傳
4 sign [saɪn] (v.) 簽署
5 sheriff [ˋʃɛrɪf] (n.)〔美〕警長

Chapter 14
My rescue

58 And now back to the two men walking across the fields to us.

The sheriff walked up to me and said: "Your name is Platt, is it?"

"Yes, master," I replied.

"Do you know that man?" he asked pointing to Northup.

I shouted out loud: "Henry B. Northup! Thank goodness."

I immediately walked towards him, but the sheriff stopped me.

"Wait," he said. "Do you have any other name than Platt?"

"Solomon Northup, master," I replied.

"Have you any family?" he asked.

"I *had* a wife, Anne, and three children: Elizabeth, Margaret and Alonzo."

"Where does that gentleman live?" he asked, again pointing[1] to Northup.

"He lives in Sandy Hill, Washington County, New York," was my reply.

59 I pushed past him and walked to my old friend. I took both his hands, and started to cry.

"Solomon," said Northup, "I'm glad to see you."

I tried to answer, but my emotions[2] prevented me from[3] speaking.

The slaves stood staring in amazement[4]. For years I had lived with them, suffered the same hardships[5], shared my grief[6] and few joys with them, but none of them knew anything of my history.

"Throw down that sack[7]," Northup said. "Your cotton-picking days are over."

Epps shook hands with the sheriff and was introduced to Northup. He invited them into the house.

When I entered, the table was covered with papers, and Northup was reading a document. Epps interrupted him.

"Platt, do you know this man?"

"Yes, master," I answered. "I've known him as long as I can remember."

"Where does he live?"

"In New York."

1 point [pɔɪnt] (v.) 指向
2 emotion [ɪ`moʃən] (n.) 情感
3 prevent from 致使無法……
4 amazement [ə`mezmənt] (n.) 吃驚；驚訝
5 hardship [`hɑrdʃɪp] (n.) 艱難；困苦
6 grief [grif] (n.) 悲傷
7 sack [sæk] (n.) 袋

60

"Did you ever live there?"

"Yes, master—born and bred[1] there."

"You were a free man, then!" he exclaimed[2]. "Why didn't you tell me that when I bought you?"

"Master Epps," I answered. "You did not ask me. Besides, I told the man that kidnapped me, and was whipped almost to death for it."

"It seems somebody wrote a letter for you. Who was it?" he demanded.

"Perhaps I wrote it myself," I answered.

"You haven't been to Marksville post office, I know that."

Epps insisted[3] that I tell him, but I did not. He made violent threats[4] against the unknown man, saying he wanted to kill the man when he found out who it was.

I walked out into the yard and met Mistress Epps. She said she was sorry to lose me, as I was better than all the other slaves, more helpful, and could play the violin for her. By the end she was in tears[5].

I said goodbye to my slave friends and to Mistress and Master Epps. I turned and walked to the carriage where Northup and the sheriff were waiting.

1 born and bred 土生土長
2 exclaim [ɪkˋsklem] (v.) 大聲叫嚷
3 insist [ɪnˋsɪst] (v.) 堅持
4 threat [θrɛt] (n.) 威脅
5 in tears 流淚

61 On Tuesday 4th January, Epps and his lawyer (a Mr Taylor), Northup, Waddill, the judge and the sheriff met in a room in Marksville. Mr Northup gave the facts about me and presented all the necessary documents. The sheriff described[1] the scene at the cotton field. They also asked me a great many questions.

Finally, Mr Taylor assured his client[2] that he was satisfied. A paper was then written and signed which declared[3] that Epps accepted my right to freedom and that he formally handed me to the authorities of New York.

Mr Northup and I immediately went to get the next steamboat to get away from there.

We were soon traveling down Red River, up which I had so unhappily been brought all those years before. I was now free, but I thought long and hard about those past years as we traveled away from that place.

For ten years I worked for Epps without reward[4]. Ten years of my endless labor helped him to get richer. Ten years I had to talk to him with eyes looking down and an uncovered head—in the way of the slave. And I got nothing back from him except undeserved[5] abuse[6] and whippings.

1 describe [dɪˋskraɪb] (v.) 描述
2 client [ˋklaɪənt] (n.) 委託人；客戶
3 declare [dɪˋklɛr] (v.) 宣布
4 reward [rɪˋwɔrd] (n.) 酬金
5 undeserved [ˏʌndɪˋzɝvd] (a.) 不當的
6 abuse [əˋbjus] (n.) 辱罵；虐待

62 He was a man who had no sense of kindness or justice. He only had a rough energy, connected to an uneducated mind and a greedy[1] nature. He was known as a "slave-breaker[2]", famous for his ability to destroy[3] the spirit of his slaves. And he was proud of this reputation[4]. He didn't think of the black man as a human being, but as a piece of living property[5], like a mule or a dog.

Slave-breaker

- Write a list of the reasons why Epps was so called.
- What do you think of Epps? Tell a friend.

1 greedy [ˋgridɪ] (a.) 貪婪的
2 breaker [ˋbrekɚ] (n.) 破壞者
3 destroy [dɪˋstrɔɪ] (v.) 毀壞；破壞
4 reputation [ˏrɛpjəˋteʃən] (n.) 名聲
5 living property 活物財產
6 obtain [əbˋten] (v.) 得到；獲得
7 board [bord] (v.) 上（車、船、飛機等）
8 register [ˋrɛdʒɪstɚ] (v.) 註冊；登記
9 circumstances [ˋsɝkəmˏstænsɪz] (n.)〔複〕情況；環境
10 proceed [prəˋsid] (v.)（沿特定路線）行進
11 transport [trænsˋpɔrt] (n.) 運輸

Chapter 15
Going home

63 We stayed in New Orleans for two days in order to obtain[6] the official legal pass stating that Henry B. Northup had the right to take me through the southern states to New York.

We then traveled to Charleston by train. When we boarded[7] the steamboat in Charleston, the Customs House officer asked Mr Northup why he had not registered[8] his slave, and he replied that he had no slave, and explained the circumstances[9]. I was worried that they might still create problems for me, but we were allowed to proceed[10], and arrived in Washington on January 17th, 1853.

Journey home

- Go back to page 30. Look at the map or at a map on the Internet to follow Solomon's journey home.
- Write a list of all the different types of transport[11] Solomon uses to get home.

64

Once we arrived in Washington we started to inquire[1] about my kidnappers. There was no way of finding information about Brown or Hamilton but we found out that Burch and Radburn were still living in Washington. So we immediately made an official complaint[2] to the police against James H. Burch for kidnapping and selling me into slavery.

Burch was arrested immediately and on January 18th there was a lengthy[3] hearing[4] before a judge in court with various witnesses[5]. During the hearing, two men spoke as witnesses for Burch, saying that he bought me legally from my owner and that it was I, together with Brown and Hamilton, who had tried to trick him!

I was not allowed to speak as a witness or to give my version[6] of the story because of the color of my skin.

In the end, on examination, Burch's books for 1841 showed no records of either the buying or selling of me under any name. Based on[7] this, the court decided that Burch had bought me innocently[8] and honestly, and so he was acquitted[9].

1 inquire [ɪn`kwaɪr] (v.) 訊問
2 complaint [kəm`plent] (n.) 控告
3 lengthy [`lɛŋθɪ] (a.) 長的；冗長的
4 hearing [`hɪrɪŋ] (n.) 審訊
5 witness [`wɪtnɪs] (n.) 證人
6 version [`vɝʒən] (n.) 版本
7 based on 以……為根據
8 innocently [`ɪnəsn̩tlɪ] (adv.) 無罪地
9 acquit [ə`kwɪt] (v.) 無罪釋放

65

I do not know what people will believe about my story of what happened in Washington twelve years ago. If I were guilty of trying to trick Burch as he stated, why would I have come back to Washington and insisted on a hearing before a judge?

I wanted everybody to know the truth, but with hindsight[1] perhaps I should have proceeded straight for home, rather than stopping in Washington to try to bring my kidnappers to justice.

At least by telling my story here, I am able to state the facts to be judged freely at last.

Northup and I left Washington and on the morning of January 22nd I went to Glen Falls, the home of Anne and our children.

It is difficult to describe the emotions of our meeting. Anne and Elizabeth hung on to me in tears. Margaret—who had been only seven years old when I left—did not remember me; she was now a married woman with a young son of her own.

Once we had calmed down a little, we sat by the fire and started talking about the thousand things which had happened in the past twelve years.

1 hindsight [ˋhaɪnd͵saɪt] (n.) 後見之明
2 truthful [ˋtruθfəl] (a.) 真實的；誠實的
3 account [əˋkaʊnt] (n.) 記述；描述
4 fiction [ˋfɪkʃən] (n.) 虛構
5 exaggeration [ɪg͵zædʒəˋreʃən] (n.) 誇張；誇大
6 wear out 耗盡
7 rest [rɛst] (v.) 安息；長眠

66 *Here, my story ends. I have no comments to make about the subject of slavery. Those who read this book can form their own opinions about it. I don't know what it was like in other states, but I can honestly say that I have given a truthful[2] account[3] of what slavery was like for me in the states I was in. This is no fiction[4], no exaggeration[5]. I am sure there are hundreds of free men who have been kidnapped and sold into slavery, and who are, at this moment, still wearing out[6] their lives on plantations in Texas and Louisiana.*

I can only speak for myself and my own suffering and be thankful that I have been able to return to a life of happiness and liberty.

I hope now to be able to live a good but simple life and then to rest[7] where my father now sleeps.

Ⓐ Personal Response

1 What did you like and dislike the most about this story?

2 Solomon ends his story saying:

> "I have no comments about the subject of slavery. Those who read this book can form their own opinions about it."

What does Solomon Northup's book tell us about slavery? What is the purpose of the book?

3 What is the message of the story? Write one sentence and then share with a friend. Then compare with another pair.

4 What did you learn from this story? Make a list and compare with the rest of the class.

5 Solomon was a slave for twelve years. What do we know about the other slaves in the story?

6 What is your reaction to the white slave owners in the story? List your reactions and compare and contrast them in pairs.

7 Speaking of the film one critic said:

> "Minds will be opened, perhaps even changed by what they see (and indeed, feel) here."

Has this story changed you in any way? Discuss with a partner.

B Comprehension

8 Tick (✓) true (T) or false (F).

- T F (a) Solomon's father was a slave all his life.
- T F (b) Solomon was born a slave.
- T F (c) Solomon's real name was Platt.
- T F (d) Before being sold as a slave, Solomon had a happy family life.
- T F (e) Solomon's first owner, William Ford, was very cruel.
- T F (f) Solomon had three owners.
- T F (g) As a slave Solomon worked as a carpenter and cotton picker.
- T F (h) Solomon never lost hope of returning to his family.

9 Correct the false sentences.

10 What do you remember from the beginning of the story? Ask and answer with a friend.

- (a) Who were the two circus men who kidnapped Solomon?
- (b) What did the circus men steal from Solomon?
- (c) Which two cities did they take him to for work?
- (d) Where was Solomon taken on the sailing ship?
- (e) Which free man did Solomon meet on the journey?
- (f) How much did William Ford pay for Solomon?

11 Put these scenes from the story in chronological order.

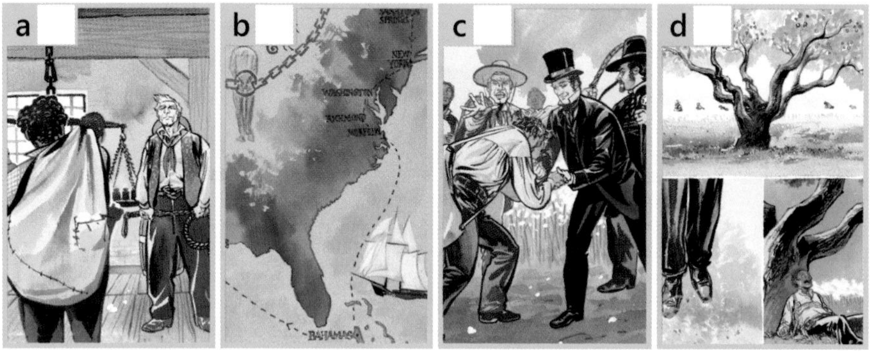

12 Write a description of what is happening in each scene. Include the place, the people, what's happening, etc.

a

b

c

d

13 What is Solomon talking about? Match the things with a sentence.

1

2

3

4
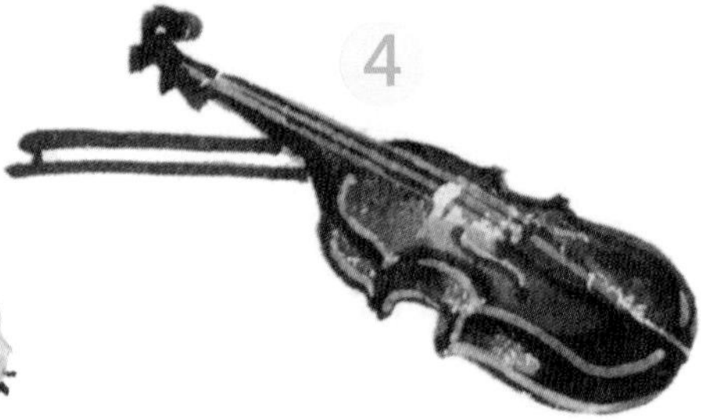

_____ (a) At the end of the day I had only forty kilos—only half the correct daily amount.

_____ (b) It seemed a sensible idea, so we went to the Customs House and got the documents.

_____ (c) And indeed, if it had not been for my beloved instrument, I don't know how I could have survived my years as a slave.

_____ (d) My main aim always was to find a way of writing to some of my friends or family.

14 When was the only time the slaves did not have to work and could enjoy themselves?

C Characters

15 Complete the sentences with the words in the box.

drunk	hang	freed	whipping	helped
debt	freedom	satisfied	cruel	

a) Henry B. Northup was a member of the family that had _______________ Solomon's father.

b) William Ford had to sell Solomon and other slaves because he was in _______________.

c) Tibeats was never _______________ with the work Solomon did.

d) One day Tibeats wanted to _______________ Solomon.

e) Epps was a very _______________ owner.

f) Epps was often _______________ and enjoyed _______________ his slaves.

g) John P. Waddill was a lawyer who _______________ Henry B. Northup find Solomon.

h) It was Bass who helped Solomon obtain his _______________.

16 Who, for you, was the worst character in the story? Who was the nicest? Give reasons for your choices and compare your choices with a friend.

17 Bass is a very important character who helps Solomon obtain his freedom. Why did Solomon think he could trust Bass with his story?

_____ (a) Because Bass was also a slave.

_____ (b) Because Bass was against slavery.

(67) **18** Listen to what Solomon says about William Ford and answer the questions.

_____ (a) What is Solomon saying here?

(1) Ford was not really religious because he had slaves.

(2) Ford felt it was right to have slaves as it was normal where he lived and most people had them.

_____ (b) What is he also saying?

(1) Where we live does not influence how most people think.

(2) Where we live influences how most people think.

19 Work with a friend. Read the following statements from the story and discuss the questions.

a

When the others said I was dying, Epps finally called the doctor. This was only because he didn't want to lose an animal worth $1,000.

↘ Who or what is the animal worth $1,000?

b

"But Epps," continued Bass, "are all men created free and equal as the Declaration of Independence says they are?" "Yes," responded Epps, "but all *men*—not slaves and monkeys."

↘ What is Epps saying here?

c

"There is a law for the slave as well as for the white man."

↘ What is Chapin trying to tell Tibeats here?

D Plot and Theme

20 Put the these events from the story in the correct order.

____ (a) Solomon is sold to William Ford.

____ (b) Solomon meets Samuel Bass, who is against slavery.

____ (c) Solomon lives as a free man in Saratoga.

____ (d) Solomon is sold to Edwin Epps.

____ (e) Solomon meets two men from a circus who kidnap and sell him.

____ (f) Solomon becomes a slave for John M. Tibeats.

____ (g) Two lawyers, Northup and Waddill, free Solomon.

____ (h) Solomon is put on a ship and taken to New Orleans.

21 Solomon speaks in detail about the typical day in a slave's life. Complete the sentences below.

(a) The working day begins at ________________.

(b) The working day ends at ________________.

(c) The break time is ________________.

(d) The amount of cotton picked per person is at least ________________.

(e) If not enough cotton, the punishment is ________________.

(f) The food eaten is ________________.

(g) What is done in the evening is to ________________.

(h) They finally get to bed ________________.

22 Solomon is telling his story in his own words. It is first-person narration. What does this mean? Tick (✓).

____ (a) It is very objective.
____ (b) It is very subjective.
____ (c) We don't have the opinions of other characters.
____ (d) We feel more distant from the author.
____ (e) We feel closer to the author.
____ (f) We may have a more detailed picture of events.

23 The story explores different aspects of humanity, what makes us human and what makes us civilized.

(a) Bass says to Epps: "There are monkeys among white people, too." What does Bass mean? Tick (✓).
☐ some white people look like monkeys
☐ some white people behave like monkeys / animals

(b) Bass also says: "These slaves are human beings." What should make us different from animals, and make us human beings? Tick (✓).
☐ how we live ☐ how we dress
☐ our brain ☐ our rules and laws

24 Prejudice and discrimination are themes in the story. Are there any prejudices in your school? Think of the following: fashion, physical appearance, and academic ability.

E Language

25 Complete this table with words connected to slavery and words against slavery.

owner abolish/abolitionist freedom
slave dealer free man master whipping
liberty punishment illegal prisoner equality

CONNECTED TO SLAVERY	AGAINST SLAVERY

26 Complete the sentences using free or freedom.

a) My name is Solomon Northup and I was born a ________ man. I lived ________ for thirty years, and then I was kidnapped and sold as a slave.

b) When old Mr Northup died (around 1800), he gave my father his ________.

c) I started doing farm work with my father from a young age, but in my ________ time, I studied, and also played the violin, which was my greatest passion.

d) The next day, they suggested I get my "________ papers," since Washington was in a slave state.

e) I longed for liberty, thinking of the thousands of miles that lay between me and the ________ of the North.

27 Change the sentences from either reported speech into direct speech or from direct speech into reported speech.

a "There is a law for the slave as well as for the white man."
Chapin told Tibeats that ______________________.

b "It's all wrong, Epps, ... I wouldn't own a slave if I were a millionaire."
Bass told Epps that ______________________.

c I begged him not to tell Epps if he could not post the letter. He said he could both post it and keep it a secret.
"______________________"

d "Why are you here? . . . Who are you?"
Bass asked Solomon ______________________.

28 These expressions in the story all use the preposition in. Match them with their meaning.

____	a in twos	1 tied to a metal cord
____	b in the wrong	2 in pairs
____	c in no fit state	3 to have made a mistake
____	d in chains	4 not physically well / strong

29 Use the expressions from Exercise **28** to complete the sentences.

a The children held hands as they walked out of the classroom ______________.

b You can't play football today. You have a high temperature and are ______________.

c I feel so sorry for that dog. It spends most of the day ______________.

d At least you're honest and admit when you're ______________.

TEST

1 Listen and tick (✓) the correct picture.

68 a

1 

2 

b

1 

2 

c

1 

2 

d

1 

2 

P **2** Choose the correct answer.

_____ (a) Who kidnapped Solomon and sold him as a slave?

1. Chapin the overseer.
2. Hamilton and Brown.
3. Waddill and Northup.
4. Peter Tanner.

_____ (b) In which U.S. city did Solomon's journey as a slave begin?

1. Boston.
2. New Orleans.
3. Washington.
4. Philadelphia.

_____ (c) What was the new name Solomon was given as a slave?

1. Lawson.
2. Manning.
3. Radburn.
4. Platt.

_____ (d) How old was Solomon when he was made a slave for twelve years?

1. Twenty-five.
2. Thirty-three.
3. Forty.
4. Twenty-nine.

_____ (e) Who finally contacted Solomon's wife for him?

1. Bass.
2. William Ford.
3. John M. Tibeats.
4. Edwin Epps.

3 Complete Solomon's thoughts. Match the sentence halves.

1. form their own opinions about it.
2. to escape through these big forests.
3. I was rescued and again became a free man.
4. long and hard about those past years.

____ (a) I lived as a slave for twelve years until ________

____ (b) I thought how impossible it would be ________

____ (c) I was now free, but I thought ________

____ (d) Those who read this book can ________

PROJECT WORK

SLAVERY

Look at this image of some slaves in a cotton plantation. Divide the class into three groups. Each group chooses a topic from below to research, preparing a presentation for the rest of the class.

Cotton picking and "The Black Belt"

What was it? Where was it?

How many slaves worked here?

Where did they come from?

Conditions on the plantations.

How much cotton was produced there and where did it go?

The abolition of slavery

When was it abolished?

How was it connected to the American Civil War?

What was the role of Abraham Lincoln?

What other important people were involved?

The legacy of slavery

Think about prejudice and discrimination between black and white Americans in recent times.
How have things improved?

How did these people contribute to the changes: Rosa Parks, Martin Luther King, John Fitzgerald Kennedy?

What was the Washington Peace March? What is the Ku Klux Klan?

Each group can choose how to present their work: either on the Interactive White Board, on a poster, as a group discussion, etc.

TRANSLATION

作者簡介

1808 年七月，所羅門．諾薩普出生於美國紐約州。他的父親原本是諾薩普家的奴隸，在當奴隸多年之後，諾薩普家還予他自由。從此以後，所羅門的家人——父親、母親和哥哥喬瑟夫——搬到附近一帶，以自由之身的身分，從事各種工作。所羅門的父親也盡量確保能夠讓兒子們接受到良好的教育。

所羅門於 1829 年結婚，以自由之身建立了家庭。但若干年後的某一天，他在尋找工作做時，遇見了兩個白人，他們設局欺騙他，在華盛頓將他販賣為奴。就這樣，所羅門過了十二年被奴役的歲月，直到律師享利．B．諾薩普將他營救出來——享利．B．諾薩普正是釋予父親自由的那個家族的成員。這本書所講述的，就是所羅門．諾薩普被奴役十二年的悲慘歲月。

美國的蓄奴可回溯至英國的殖民時代，在 1776 年《獨立宣言》發表之後，有十三個州認可蓄奴。最初從非洲被帶往美國的黑人，他們在美國被販賣為奴，在奴役州的菸草、蔗糖或棉花農場上工作。在奴役州，蓄奴是合法的；在自由州，蓄奴是非法的。奴隸沒有權利，在白人奴隸主的眼裡，他們不過比動物或機械來得好一些。一直到 1865 年，美國所有的州才廢除了奴隸制度。

本書簡介

《自由之心：為奴十二年》講述自由之人所羅門．諾薩普的經歷。他從 1841 年被非法販賣為奴開始，最初是威廉．福特的奴隸，接著在約翰．M．提畢茲那裡經歷一段愈來愈殘酷的境遇，再後來是愛德恩．伊普司，所羅門最後從他那裡被營救出來，那一年是 1853 年。

所羅門清楚描繪自己奴役歲月的景況，那是無止盡的勞動、不公平的對待，奴隸被視為財產，毫無人道可言。本書詳述奴隸每天要幹的活，細說所羅門的各種遭遇，包括逃亡的企圖。

1853 年五月，所羅門．諾薩普出版了他的故事，由大衛．威爾森所編輯。所羅門期盼讀者能對美國奴隸州的黑奴處境有所知曉。在前言，編輯大衛．威爾森表示，他堅信所羅門被奴役十二年的經歷是千真萬確的。他盡可能做了查明，即使無法事事都得到驗證。

威爾森表示，在所羅門被奴役的歲月裡，所羅門經歷過多位奴隸主，而這恰恰是他的「好運道」。這些奴隸主，有的展現了人道，有的只有殘忍可言。的確，所羅門談到這些人的時候，不是帶著感激，就是帶著痛苦。

2012 年，本書被拍成電影，由史提夫．麥昆執導。本片多在路易斯安那州的紐奧良拍攝，在當年夏天，使用了四座史上知名的棉花田農場當作拍攝地點。電影於 2013 年發行，並榮獲了多項主要大獎。

第一章　我的出身

P. 15

我的名字叫所羅門·諾薩普，我生來是一個自由之身。我自由地活了三十年，後來卻遭到綁架，被販賣為奴隸。我以奴隸之身，又過了十二個年頭。最後，我被營救出來，重獲自由之身。這是我的親身經歷。

我的父親是一位奴隸，為紐約州的諾薩普家賣命。一八○○年左右，諾薩普老爺去世，他許給我父親自由之身。我父親後來隨了這家人的姓，成了明塔斯·諾薩普。諾薩普一家人向來就關心我們，又蒙名律師享利·B·諾薩普所惠，他是諾薩普家族的親戚，所以我現在才得以重獲自由。

我父親被給予自由之後，便帶著母親和兄長，在紐約州幾處不同的農場幫忙幹農活。

P. 16

一八○八年七月，我呱呱墜地。我們一家人生活順心，多虧父親的理念和教導，比起大多數的非裔美國人，我們接受了較好的教育。

父親也常常跟我們提起他以前當奴隸的前塵往事。他當時所受到的對待，並不像一般奴隸那樣悲慘，但是他認為很重要的是我們要去了解奴隸的體制，明白這對我們的同胞來說是怎麼一回事。

我小時候就開始幫父親做些農活，閒暇時，我會讀書，也會拉拉小提琴，這可是我最大的樂趣。一八二○年，父親撒手人寰。

一八二九年，我娶了安·漢普頓，她也是自由之身，是一位多種族混血兒。婚後，我接了各種苦力的工作，以便補貼家用。我常得為這些活四處奔波，有一次還甚至到過加拿大。

最後，我們終於攢了足夠的錢，可以買塊農地，之後我便開始務農。安的工作是廚子，而地方上的夜間舞會常需要我去拉小提琴。到目前為止，靠著我們兩個人的兩份收入，有一段時間我們過著簡單而舒適的生活。

為了想掙更多的錢，一八三四年，我們搬到紐約州的薩拉托加溫泉市。我的工作是駕馬車，安則是在附近一家旅館擔任廚子。此外，我也拉拉小提琴或是接一些臨時的苦力，來賺取外快。

P. 18

在這段時間裡，我經常看到奴隸的身影，他們陪著主人從南方過來。他們穿著得體，衣食無缺，看起來日子相對好過些。不過，在和他們聊過他們的處境之後，我發現他們都想成為自由之身。有的還說他想逃跑，但是害怕萬一被抓到，又得回到奴隸主的身邊，後果不堪設想。

和他們的這些談話，讓我更確知了父親所說過的奴役的邪惡本質，還有每個人對自由的需求。

我和安一直待在薩拉托加溫泉市，直到一八四一年的年初。我們生活愜意，但不算富裕，所以每一個掙錢的機會都很重要。在這段時間，我們有了三個孩子——伊麗莎白、瑪格麗特和亞倫佐——他們給我們帶來了很大的幸福。

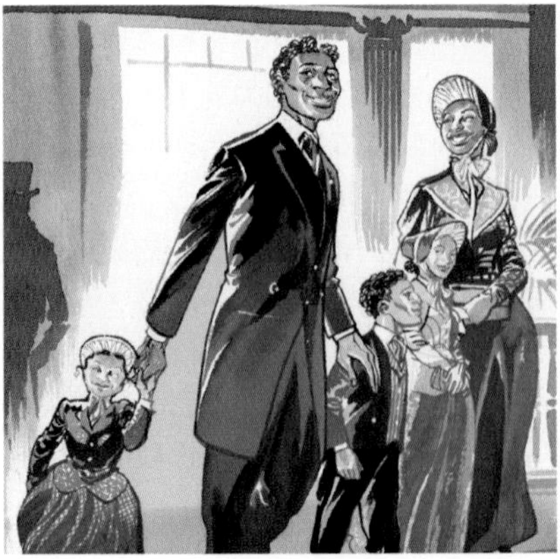

第二章　兩位陌生人

P. 19

一八四一年三月，安帶著孩子們去沙地山做廚房的工作。當我在薩拉托加尋找工作時，遇到了兩名衣冠楚楚的白人，他們一個叫漢彌頓，一個叫布朗。他們是馬戲團的人，從華盛頓市來的，這次是私下來這一帶出遊，偶而做做表演。他們要一路前往紐約，表演時需要有人幫忙演奏，便找我說，他們會每天算給我一塊錢，每表演一場另外支付三塊錢，外加從紐約返回薩拉托加的車馬費。

我立刻接下這份優渥的差事。我琢磨這段旅程不長，便沒給安捎短信，只是帶上小提琴和一套換洗的衣物。

我們搭馬車前往奧本尼，在傍晚時分抵達。他們做了場表演，我拉小提琴。布朗做了拋球雜技、在繩上跳舞、表演腹語，並耍了些魔術把戲，漢彌頓則守在門口。這次觀看的人寥寥無幾，幾乎分文未進。

P. 20

短信

- 你要去某地時，你通常會怎麼做？請勾選。
  - ☐ 留個字條。
  - ☐ 告訴某人。
  - ☐ 寄個簡訊。
  - ☐ 打電話跟某人說。
- 要去某地時，為什麼跟別人告知去處，總是比較好？請作小組討論。

隔天早上，我們早早便啟程。他們決定不再做表演，而是一路直接前往紐約。到了紐約，他們又找我一起去華盛頓，加入他們的馬戲團，說會付給我一筆可觀的錢，於是我答應了。

第二天，他們建議我先去辦個「自由之身的證明」，因為華盛頓位於蓄奴州。這看起來是個明智的想法，我們便來到海關大樓，拿到文件證明，然後前往華盛頓。

布朗和漢彌頓對我始終極為彬彬有禮，並且待我寬厚。那個晚上，他們給了我四十三塊，並向我道歉，表示他們沒有依照承諾做表演。

P. 21

他們帶我去參觀國會大廈、總統宮和其他景點，我們時不時會停下來喝一杯，他們總會遞上酒給我。等我們回到旅館的時候，我開始感覺不適，連去吃晚餐也沒辦法。我頭痛欲裂，無法入睡。我的口很渴，但喝水並沒有讓我舒緩些。

蓄奴州

- 找出「蓄奴州」和「自由州」的資料。
- 翻回到第五頁，尋找定義，並使用網路來輔助。請作小組討論。

P. 22

稍後，他們說我得去看醫生，於是我便被帶往街上。之後，發生了什麼事，我渾然不知。

等我甦醒過來時，只有我孤身一人，四周一片漆黑，而且我被戴上了鐐銬。我感到很虛弱，坐在一張矮凳上。我的雙手被銬著，腳踝上圈著金屬腳鐐，鐐上的鐵鍊連接到地板的一個鐵環上。

我無法站起身。這裡是哪裡？布朗和漢彌頓去哪裡了？我怎麼這樣被囚禁起來了？我的盤纏和「自由之身的證明文件」，都被拿走了。我意識到，我一定是被綁架了。我感到可怕的孤獨與絕望，不禁痛哭失聲。

第三章　鐐銬與黑暗

P. 24

某個時刻，門被打開了，光線瀉入房間。我終於看到自己身置何處——空蕩蕩的地窖，鋪著木頭地板，還有我坐著的這張板凳。

兩個男人走進房間，他們是詹姆士·H·伯奇和伊班·拉本。伯奇年約四十，他塊頭高大，孔武有力，一張臉冷酷而狡猾，他在華盛頓是臭名昭著的奴隸販子，拉本則是他手下的頭頭。

「你感覺怎樣？」伯奇問道。

我說我人很不舒服，並且問他為什麼我被關了起來。他說，他剛把我買下，我是他的奴隸了，他要把我送到紐奧良。

我大聲喊道，我是自由之身，是薩拉托加的居民，家有妻兒，我姓諾薩普。他卻跟我說，我不是自由之身，而且我來自喬治亞州。

我重申，我是自由之身，並且吩咐他解開我的鐐銬。

他頓時大發雷霆，罵我是騙子，說我是從喬治亞州的主人家中逃跑的奴隸。接著，他要拉本把拍子和九尾鞭拿來。

P. 25

拍子是木頭做成的板子，九尾鞭是分有多束的粗繩，每束繩子的末端都綁著一個結。接著，他們扒下我的衣服，把我從凳子上揪下來。伯奇開始用拍子打我的身體，然後停下來，問我是不是還要嘴硬說自己是自由之身。我說是。於是他又開始揮打，而且下手更快、更重。

這樣的戲碼重複好幾次，最後，拍子打裂了，而我仍不屈服，不肯謊說自己是奴隸。於是，他拿起九尾鞭，開始往我身上抽。這鞭子打起來更加疼痛，我渾身痛如火燒，感覺自己全身只剩骨頭而已。

最後，拉本說再打下去也是白搭，伯奇這才停下手。伯奇吼道，說我要是敢再說自己是自由之身，或是被綁架了之類的話，就有更嚴厲的懲罰等著瞧。接著，他們解下我手腕上的鐐銬，然後走出房間，鎖上門，再度把我留在黑暗之中。

P. 26

後來，拉本走回來，帶來一小塊炸豬排、一片麵包和一杯水。他勸我別再說自己是自由之身了，除非我想再討打一頓。接著，他去掉我腳上的鐐銬，稍微打開安上了鐵條的窗戶，然後又留下我一個人。

這時，我身體變得非常疼痛，只要稍微一動，就痛苦難忍。那天夜裡，我躺在空無一物的硬地板上，沒有枕頭，沒有被褥。

想像

- 你能想像所羅門的感受嗎？
- 布朗和漢彌頓對所羅門幹了什麼好事？

拉本都會帶來同樣的食物，一天兩回。我一直很口渴，身體的傷口不容我維持某個姿勢太久。我常常想起我的妻子和孩子，這讓我忍不住啜泣。不過，我的意志還沒有崩潰，我想了各種逃跑的方法，我不相信有人可以如此不公不義地對待別人。我仍盼望著，等伯奇知道我確實是自由之身時，他大概就會放我走；或者，布朗和漢彌頓可能會來尋找我。

P. 27

過了幾天之後，他們准許我可以走出到院子裡。我在院子裡看到了三個奴隸：一個十歲大的男孩，兩個二十多歲的小伙子。我們跟他們交談，略知了他們的來歷。

他們給我們每個人一張馬用的毯子，在往後的十二年裡，這是我唯一可以擁有的寢具。

這種地方稱為奴隸場。在威廉斯奴隸場待了兩個星期之後，那個男孩的母親和妹妹也被帶了進來。他們很高興能再重逢，儘管母親伊麗莎意識到他們之後可能就要永別了。

聯想

- 將這一頁和動物有關，而不是和人有關的字劃出來。
- 這述說了這些奴隸受到什麼樣的待遇？請作小組討論。

第四章　南方之行

P. 28

不久後，一個半夜裡，伯奇和拉本命令我們起床，要我們搭上一艘汽船，我們便開始了前往紐奧良的漫長旅程。他們把我們塞進下層的貨艙，我們沿波多馬克河而下。隔天日中之前，船來到了阿維亞溪。伯奇要我們跟他上一輛貨車，然後駛往維吉尼亞州的首府里士滿，我們被帶到當地的古丁奴隸場。顯然，伯奇和古丁是舊識。

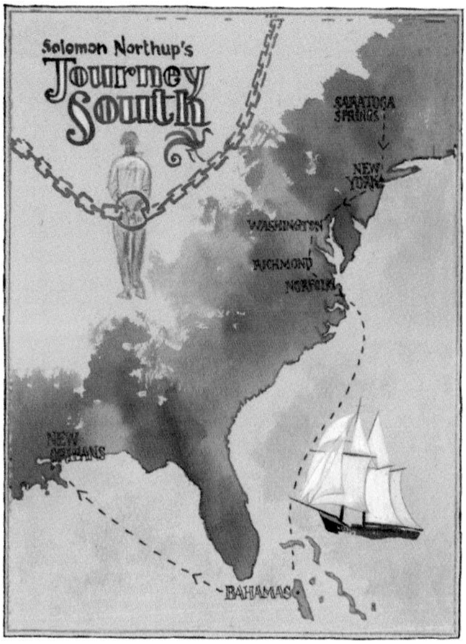

隔天下午，我們兩兩並排地穿越過里士滿的街道，走向一艘大帆船「奧爾良號」。這時，我們四十個人都上了船，然後被鎖在貨艙裡。

我們來到諾福克市，在這裡有一艘比較小的船開過來，又送來四個奴隸上船：兩個男孩，一個女孩，和一個叫作亞瑟的男人。亞瑟到來時，不肯就範於押送的人，一邊嚷著喊冤，他的一張臉被打得很慘。我後來得知，他和我一樣，原本是自由之身。他是晚上在街上時被一幫人抓到，之後被押進奴隸場待了幾天。

P. 29

我們這趟船運旅程很漫長，因為天候惡劣，我們常常暈船，一直到通過大巴哈馬淺灘，情況才好轉。

在我們船上，有一個人染到了天花，他在我們抵達紐奧良之前就病死了。日子很難熬，白天裡我們有一整天的活要幹，晚上則把我們都鎖進貨艙裡。

有一天，一個叫作約翰·曼寧的水手和我交談。我跟他說我是自由之身，遭人綁架，他表示他想幫助我。我請他幫我找來筆墨和紙張，以便寫信給亨利·B·諾薩普先生，尋求援助。

於是當天夜裡，我躲到甲板的小船上，和曼寧碰面。我寫好信，然後把信交給他。他允諾會在紐奧良把信寄出去。

P. 31

日後，我得知諾薩普先生確實收到了信件，並把信呈給了當局，只不過因為無人知曉我究竟身處何方，所以他們決定暫時擱置，等獲得進一步的消息之後，再作打算。

而亞瑟，他幸運多了，當我們最終抵達紐奧良時，有兩個人來釋放了他。綁架他的人已經被繩之以法，而在和船長談過之後，亞瑟便和那兩個人一同下船離開了。我為他感到欣慰，但這也令我更感到絕望與孤寂。

在紐奧良，希非·費曼先生來接走了伯奇的奴隸。一開始，出現了一些混亂，因為他是用「普雷特」這個名字來叫我，伯奇是這樣跟他報上我的名字的。於是，在接下來十二年的奴隸生涯當中，人們就用普雷特這個名字來叫喚我。

我們被帶往費曼奴隸場，這裡和里士滿的古丁奴隸場很相像。

第二天，費曼給我們都換上簡單款式的新衣服。有很多買主上門，他們檢驗我們，費曼說我們品質良好。一位紐奧良的年長紳士相中了我，想要我幫他駕馬車，但他不肯付到一千五百元，這是費曼對我的開價。

P. 32

就在那天晚上，我們這些從奧爾良號下來的奴隸都病倒了。我跟醫生說了羅伯特染上天花的事情。伊麗莎、她的孩子、一個叫哈利的男人，還有我，我們被送往城外的一間大醫院。我病情嚴重，心想自己就要死了。不過，我挨過來了，兩個星期之後，我和其他人一起返回費曼的奴隸場。疾病讓我們虛弱很多，但我們現在已經準備好待價而沽了。

一些時日後，來了一位穿著體面的中年男人。他詢問我們在行的事，最後他同意用一千元買下我，用九百元買下哈利，用七百元買下伊麗莎。伊麗莎聽到之後，非常的哀愁，因為她不想和孩子們分開，但她莫可奈何。到目前為止，據我所知，她還不曾有過孩子們的消息，儘管她日日夜夜都在説著孩子們的事。

第五章　福特和提畢茲

P. 34

我們被帶上魯道夫號汽船，沿密西西比河而上。我們的主人叫作威廉·福特，住在紅河岸的大松林，那裡是路易斯安那州的腹地。他是個宗教信仰很虔誠的人，一個蓄奴的人會是個宗教信仰虔誠人，聽起來可能有些奇怪，但是周遭社會的本質蒙蔽了他，讓他看不到蓄奴的不公不義。不過，他是一個好主人，他的奴隸也算是幸運能夠有他這樣一個主人。

兩天後，我們在亞歷山卓下了汽船，搭馬車朝大松林行駛了十八哩路。最後的十二哩路，我們用步行的才抵達。

福特的宅邸很大，他經營各種林業，他在那時候還很富有。他們要我們進去我們的小木屋，不久我們便在地板上睡覺。入睡前，我琢磨著，要穿越這些大森林逃出去，希望是何等的渺茫。

P. 35

第二天早上，福特老爺喊管家奴隸露絲的聲音，把我驚醒了，他要露絲去幫他的孩子們穿衣服。另一位女奴莎麗去牧場擠牛奶，年輕的廚房奴隸約翰則負責準備食物。

我和哈利到院子裡四周走走，瞧瞧我們的新家。我們後來還遇見了露絲的丈夫沃頓。福特要我和哈利跟著沃頓一起去松林裡堆木和伐木，這個餘夏，這就是我們一直在做的工作。

到了星期日，福特會把奴隸都集合到宅邸旁邊，然後閱讀《聖經》，並解釋給我們聽。

到了秋天，我在福特的宅邸四周工作。我也幫一個請來的木匠，修繕一個房間的天花板。木匠的名字叫約翰·M·提畢茲，他個子矮小，脾氣暴躁，沒有受過教育，和福特老爺完全是相反典型的人。

一八四二年的冬天，因為威廉·福特老爺幫弟弟做保人的緣故，財務上不幸陷入困境。福特也拖欠了提畢茲一大筆工錢，提畢茲蓋了棉花田那邊的房子，於是福特不得不把一些奴隸賣掉。我的木工活因為不亞於木匠，所以我也被賣給了提畢茲。

P. 36

我的身價因為高於債務，福特就採用動產抵押的方式，用我抵了四百美元。也多虧這份抵押，保住了我的性命，故事稍後你就會知道。

我先跟著提畢茲，前往二十七哩外的福特農場，把還沒完工的房子蓋好。我碰到了伊麗莎，她現在在那裡工作。她變得憔悴消瘦，依舊極度思念著孩子。

我一大早就上工，一直忙到夜晚，但提畢茲永遠不滿意。在蓋那些房子的期間，我做了一件事情，足以讓我在這一州被處死。

提畢茲要我某天起個大早，去找福特農場的監工查賓，跟他要一箱不同大小的釘子。查賓是個好心人，我去找他時，他跟我說，提畢茲如果要不同尺寸的釘子，他晚點會送過來，要我先使用現有的釘子。查賓說完就騎上馬，去田裡巡查奴隸的工作。我便走向建築物，開始手上的活。

太陽升起時，提畢茲現身來查看我的工作。

「我昨天晚上不是跟你說過，要去跟查賓拿不同小大的釘子嗎？」他問。

P. 38

「是的，老爺，我去要過了。監工說，他晚一點會幫你要到另一個尺寸的釘子，但是他現在還在田裡。」

提畢茲瞧了瞧釘子，然後氣沖沖地走向我，大喊道：「該死的，我還以為你有腦子！」

「老爺，我依您吩咐的做了，監工說……」

但提畢茲逕自跑進屋內，提了查賓的長鞭過來。一開始我很害怕，但恐懼瞬間轉為怒火，我不計後果地就是不想挨打。

他朝我走過來，命令我脫掉衣服。

「提畢茲先生，我不脫。」我直視他的臉說道。

他跳到我面前，一隻手扼住我的喉嚨，另一隻手舉起鞭子。在鞭子落在我身上之前，我往下抓住他的腳踝，朝他一推，他便跌在地上。

我抓起他的一隻腳，靠在我胸前，他的頭部和肩膀只能貼在地上，接著我一腳踩在他的脖子上，他便完全被我制止住。

他掙扎著，大聲嚷著要宰了我。我奪過他手中的鞭子，用鞭柄往他抽了好幾下。查賓聽到提畢茲的尖叫聲，從田裡騎馬趕回來，我於是一腳把提畢茲踢開。他站起身來，我們兩個人不發一語地對視著。

P. 39

「怎麼回事？」查賓看到我們兩個人，問道。

「提畢茲老爺因為我沒有使用不同尺寸的釘子，所以要鞭打我。」我回答。

查賓開始說道：「我是這裡的監工，是我要普雷特先用現有的釘子，晚一點我就會弄到不同尺寸的釘子。這不是他的錯。提畢茲先生，等我田裡的事處理好了，就去弄別的釘子過來，這樣你明白嗎？」

提畢茲沒有作聲，只是揮揮拳頭，氣炸了地朝屋子走去。查賓也跟著走過去，接著是一陣激烈的爭論。

我待在原地不動，不久，提畢茲走出房子，騎上馬離開。查賓朝我走過來，要我哪兒也別去。他說，我的主人提畢茲先生是個無賴，大概不久就會有麻煩上門。

接下來的一個鐘頭裡，我陷入悲慘和恐懼之中，意識到自己闖下了大禍。我，一個不幸的黑奴，攻擊了一個白人，而那個白人是我的主人。

提畢茲回來的時候，多帶了兩個男人。他們下馬，手上提著兩條長鞭和一條長繩。

「雙手交併。」提畢茲命令道。

P. 40

「老爺，你不用綁我，我已經準備好要跟你走。」我回答。

但他們三個人還是捆住我的雙手雙腳，讓我無法動彈。接著，提畢茲綁了一個套索，套在我的頸子上。我看到查賓站在房子的門邊。我一陣絕望，覺得自己死定了。

「現在，我們要在哪裡把這奴隸吊死？」提畢茲的一個同夥問。

「就那棵桃子樹吧。」另一個人提議道。

他們於是把我拖往桃子樹，但這時候，查賓兩手各握著一把手槍，朝我們走過來，説道：「先生們，我有幾句話要説，所以聽著，你們有誰敢再挪動這個奴隸半吋，誰就沒命。首先，沒理由他要這樣被對待，沒有人比普雷特更忠心的了。你，提畢茲，這件事錯是錯在你身上。你是個無賴，你早上被打，那是你活該。再來，我是這裡的監工，這裡由我作主，我的職責是保護威廉·福特的利益。他用普雷特抵押了四百美元，你要是把他吊死，他就會蒙受損失。在錢付清之前，你無權取他的性命。怎麼説你都沒有這個權利，法律對付奴隸，也對付白人。你這樣無異於是殺人犯。」

P. 41

查賓轉身對著那兩個同夥的，他們是附近田地的監工，説道：「你們兩個，滾！」

兩個人沒吭聲，上了馬背便離開。

提畢茲顯然是忌憚查賓，他沒帶種地摸摸鼻子離開，騎馬尾隨同夥而去。

接著，查賓喚來另一個奴隸勞森，説道：「勞森，騎上那頭跑得最快的棕色騾子，用最快的速度去松林，請你的福特老爺立刻過來。跟他説，他們想宰了普雷特。現在，快去！」

查賓

- 查賓在這裡是如何搭救普雷特（所羅門）的？翻回到第 36 頁看看。

第六章　熾烈的太陽

P. 42

我在灼熱的太陽底下站了一整天，被緊縛的繩子綁得很痛，動彈不得。查賓站在他的屋子旁，望著我看。顯然地，他心忖提畢茲會來去搭更多的人回來。我猜想，他是要讓福特親眼見到我被提畢茲整成什麼樣子。

傍晚時分，福特到來了。查賓去見他，兩人簡短談了幾句後，他朝我走過來。

「可憐的普雷特，你看起來很不妙。」他只對我説了這麼一句話。

「謝天謝地，福特老爺，你總算來了。」我回答。

他割斷綁在我手腳上的繩索，然後把我脖子上的套索取下來。我想走動看看，但跌了個跤。

福特朝屋子走回去，當他來到屋子前的時候，提畢茲和兩個同夥騎馬回來了。他們談了許久，接著三個人又再度離開，顯然是談得不歡而散。

P. 43

我爬進小木屋，躺了下來。我的狀況很不好，稍微一動就痛苦難當。不久，別的奴隸從田裡回來，伊麗莎和瑪麗給我煎了一些玉蜀黍，煮了咖啡。

他們問我發生了什麼事，我說明了始末，勞森也講了他趕去松林的事。大夥都很同情我，說提畢茲真是狠心，但願福特老爺可以把我贖回去。

這時，查賓出現在小木屋門口，他說：「普雷特，你今晚睡大宅的地板。」他怕提畢茲早上回來把我幹掉。

我擔心會發生不測，再加上身體的痛楚，我這一晚沒怎麼睡。

第二天早上，我起床困難。吃過早餐後，我出門幹活。我感到加諸在我身上的為奴悲哀。日復一日的長時工作，受別人的辱罵，睡在硬邦邦的地板上，吃粗劣的食物，最不堪的是要為惡人工作，一直活在恐懼當中。

我渴望自由。我琢磨，隔在我和自由北方之間，是數千哩的距離。

P. 44

那天稍後，福特回到松林。我一直對提畢茲提心吊膽，生怕他隨時都可能會對我怎麼樣。不過，他似乎都跟我保持距離，只有在必要時才會過來查看我的工作。

這星期，我一直忙著的房子完工了。提畢茲跟我說，他把我出租給彼得．坦納，那是福特老爺的哥哥，在河的對岸有一塊農場。

我在另一位叫邁爾斯的木工手下工作。能夠暫時擺脫提畢茲，我很高興。當我來到這邊時，我發現大家都耳聞了我的事，包括我為福特做事時表現出色，還有我出手打提畢茲的事。不過，坦納警告我要安分點。

之後我在邁爾斯的手下工作了一個月，我們對彼此都感到滿意。

工作

- 在工作場所，為什麼尊重和合作很重要？請分組討論。

第七章　我的逃亡

P. 46

我被送回福特的農場，提畢茲正在那裡製作軋棉機。這裡離大宅有一些距離，所以通常都只有我單獨和提畢茲在工作。我記得查賓說過，提畢茲想找機會對我下手，所以我大部分的時間都神經緊繃。

第三天早上，當查賓出差去塵尼市時，提畢茲的火爆脾氣又發作了。

那時我在刨木板，他站在工作臺的旁邊。

「你刨得不夠深。」他說。

「這和線對起來剛好。」我回答。

「你胡扯。」他吼道。

「好的，主人，既然您這麼說，我再刨深一點。」我和氣地說。

我照辦，但他又吼說我這下子刨太深了。他開始羞辱我，我靜靜地站著，心裡很害怕，不知如何是好。他愈來愈火大，最後他拿起一個短柄的小斧頭，對著我衝過來，説要劈開我的腦袋。

P. 47

這是生死存亡的時刻，我朝他跳過去，奪下他手上的斧頭，遠遠扔到一邊。他氣惱不已，撿起一根又長又粗的木棍，就朝著我撲過來。我把他推倒在地上，又奪走他手上的木棍，丟在一旁。

他站起來，要跑去撿地上的一根斧

頭，我於是朝他的後背撲上去，制止了他。我內心有一個聲音，要我把他給殺了，但我也知道殺人要償命。可是另一方面，只要他活著，他就會要我死。我唯一能做的，就是逃走。

我將提畢茲推倒在地上，然後躍過圍牆，飛快地穿過農場，路過棉花田。我在這裡爬上一座高圍牆，回頭眺望，望見提畢茲正騎上他的馬，一路疾馳。

如今，我的結局將會如何？誰能幫得上我？我應該往哪裡去？不久，我看到提畢茲和另外兩個人正朝著我的方向騎過來，後面跟著八隻到十隻左右的狗。我知道那是專門用來追捕奴隸的狗，從牠們猛烈的吠叫聲中，我知道牠們就在我身後不遠的地方。

P. 48

我朝著沼澤地狂奔而去，恐懼激發出我的力量。我聽到狗離我愈來愈近。我衝進河水中時，上氣不接下氣。

我知道，在水中我的味道大概就沒有了，能夠讓狗混淆。謝天謝地，我不久來到一條寬闊的河中，便游了過去。我的味道沒了，狗追蹤不到，跟不上來。

我現在身處大沼澤區。這裡長滿不同種類的高大樹木，綿延數哩。在這裡生存的，只有熊、野貓和爬蟲類動物。我的舉手投足都得小心翼翼，因為這裡到處都是毒蛇，水中也潛伏著鱷魚。

P. 49

我最後聽到狗的聲音，是在下午兩點左右。現在，蛇和鱷魚更讓我提心吊擔。

我緩緩穿越沼澤，我知道我一步步接近人們居住的區域，便又憂心起來。沒有通行證，隨便一個白人都可以把我抓起來送進牢裡，等主人出面來把我認領回去。我分不清自己最害怕的，究竟是狗、是鱷魚，還是人類。

月亮升起來之後，我變更了計畫。我開始朝北方走，而不是南方。我向威廉·福特宅邸旁的松林移動，我想在那裡會安全些。

P. 50

我的衣服磨破，手上、臉上、身上到處都是在樹林裡被劃傷的傷痕，腳上的一隻鞋子也掉了，全身上下都是污泥和灰塵。終於，我來到了乾地上，我知道我就在大松林周圍的某個地方了。

破曉時分，我來到一塊空地上，有一個老爺和奴隸們正在那裡獵野豬。我知道白人有可能把我抓去關，便選擇直接朝白人走過去，臉上裝出一副凶神惡煞的樣子。我逕自走向白人，直瞪著他的眼睛。

「威廉·福特住哪兒？」我粗魯地問道。

「他住的地方離這裡六哩遠，你往那邊那兩棵大松樹走去，會碰到德州公路，然後左轉，一直走就會到威廉·福特家了。」他回答。

我按照他報的路走，還沒不到八點，我就來到福特老爺的家了。我找到了福特，跟他說了來龍去脈。他聽我道來，憐憫地跟我說話。

他們給我端來食物，之後我進到小木屋裡睡覺，覺得鬆了好大一口氣。

第八章　伊普司

P. 51

隔天下午，我來到福特太太的花園，那裡長滿美麗的花朵和水果。我想做些什麼來報答福特一家人，便開始著手拔除花園裡的雜草。福特太太走出來誇獎我，但是說我的身體狀況還不適合勞動。我跟她說這活兒很輕鬆，請她放心，還說能為這樣一位好心的太太工作，實在令人感到愉悅。因此，接下來的三天，我都在她的花園裡清除雜草。

到了第四天早上，福特老爺要我跟他一起去沼澤區。在路上，我們碰到了提畢茲。他沒有跟我講話，只是騎在馬上和福特並排走，一邊談著話。

福特跟他說了我驚險的經歷，提畢茲提到他是怎麼追捕我的，他心想我已經命喪沼澤地了。福特跟提畢茲說，他待我太壞了，錯都要歸到他的頭上。

P. 52

「提畢茲先生，很清楚的，你不能和普雷特湊在一塊兒，你看他不順眼，想要他的命。這他也知道，所以才逃命。你一定要把他賣掉，或是外租給別人。你要是不這麼做，我就要從你那裡把人帶走。」

我回到了農場。隔天早上，我碰到提畢茲，他跟我說，他已經把我賣給一個叫做愛德恩．伊普司的人。

我們直接來到伊普司的農場。伊普司檢查了我一番，問了我一些奴隸買家慣例會問的問題。我不再是提畢茲的財產，這讓我覺得很脫解。

我想，新主人一定會是個好轉的契機。

愛德恩．伊普司的身高六尺多，塊頭很大，一頭淺色頭髮，藍眼珠，顴骨很高，有一個大鼻子。他講話的樣子就感覺沒受過什麼教育，舉止也令人討厭。他還嗜好杯中物，一喝醉，就會吵吵鬧鬧地和奴隸一起跳舞，不然就是對奴隸抽鞭子。他清醒時，寡言而狡猾，會出其不意地讓鞭子落在奴隸身上不尋常的地方。

他這時租了一塊叫霍夫包的農場，那裡靠近河口，是跟妻子的叔父租來的，用來種植棉花。

在伊普司主人的田地，一整年裡，犁地、栽種、摘棉花、採玉蜀黍、拔舊的作物，這些活兒就佔據了奴隸絕大部分的時間。

P. 53

在採收棉花的季節，所有的奴隸每一天起碼要摘八十五公斤的棉花，儘管有些人可以採收得更多，而如果採收量不足，就要吃鞭子。

我們每天從日出工作到日沒，中間只有十五分鐘的休息。當監工一喊停工，棉花便開始秤重。

奴隸要前去秤重時，都是心驚膽戰的。要是採收不足，就有得受；要是採收過量，那明天也要採收同樣的量才可以，所以兩邊都不對。

在秤重和鞭打完之後，奴隸要扛著自己的籃子到棉花房，繼續其他的活兒，餵騾子、餵豬、砍柴，點著燭火把這些事做完。

最後，我們才筋疲力竭地回到我們的小木屋。我們還得生火，準備晚餐和明天的午餐。我們吃的東西只有玉蜀黍和培根肉，這些東西每個星期天早上發一次。等這些食物都張羅好，往往是大半夜了。

P. 55

奴隸睡覺時，也是戰戰兢兢的，生怕隔天早上會睡過頭，那樣要吃二十下鞭子。在我跟著伊普司的時間裡，我睡在寬三十公分的板子上，用一截木頭當枕頭，蓋一張粗劣的毯子。

天亮前一個小時，號角就會響起，奴隸們便起床。他們會在一個葫蘆裡灌滿水，在另一個葫蘆裡塞進冷培根肉和玉米餅，當午餐食用，然後又匆匆趕去田地。天亮之後，奴隸只要被看到還待在木屋裡，就要挨打。

棉花的採收，從八月底一直持續到一月。接著，是玉蜀黍採收的季節。在當地，玉蜀黍不是重要作物，主要是用來餵豬，並供給奴隸作食物。八月時，會把莖稈上的葉子剝掉，給牲畜作草糧；玉蜀黍剩下的部分，通常到二月份才會採收。

奴隸

- 請一一列出，在伊普司的農場裡，奴隸每天要做的不同事情有哪些。
- 普雷特的新主人，有讓情況好轉嗎？和夥伴討論。

第九章　鞭打與跳舞

P. 56

我初到伊普司老爺這裡時，得了熱病，身體變得很虛弱，而且消瘦了下來。我得一直工作，但我發現我的手腳就是快不起來，所以挨了監工的鞭子。到了九月，我終於連木屋都爬不出來了。老爺和太太沒給我藥，也沒來關心，只有老廚子有時會過來看我，給我煮點玉米咖啡或是培根肉。

等到別人說我快死了，伊普司這才叫了醫生，而這只是因為他不想損失一頭價值一千元的動物。

醫生說，這是氣候引起的，要我不能吃肉，其他的東西也只能吃一點點。這樣吃了幾個星期後，我康復了些，伊普司便要我到棉花田裡上工。

P. 57

我沒有採收棉花的經驗，我發現這活兒真不好幹。這一天下來，我採收了四十公斤，才一日採收量的一半而已。伊普司看我是新手，便饒過我。不過，不管我怎麼練習，或是吃多少鞭子，我的採收量就是增加不了。

伊普司說，把我帶去棉花田，真是丟臉。後來，我就去伐木、搬運木材、扛棉花去秤重，做其他各種必要的活兒。

很罕見有哪一天是不抽鞭子的，這是在棉花秤重完開始進行的。受罰的奴隸要把衣服扒掉，臉朝下地趴在地上，接受鞭打。像在棉花袋裡發現枯葉這樣的小過，要吃二十五下鞭子，這是最基本的鞭打次數；被發現偷懶怠工的奴隸，要吃一百下鞭子；吵架滋事，打兩百下；要是想逃跑的話，打五百下，外加放狗群咬。

在伊普司的農場上，整個採收棉花的季節裡，鞭子的劈啪聲和奴隸的慘叫聲，會從天黑之後一直響到睡覺時間。

P. 58

每次伊普司只要去洪司市回來，就是酩酊大醉。他會摔房子裡所有的盤子、椅子，然後去庭院裡四處晃，見人就抽鞭子，或是吩咐來場音樂和舞蹈。

因為提畢茲跟他說過我會拉小提琴，所以我常被叫去演奏。只要伊普司跳舞的興致一來，我們所有人就要集合到宅邸的大廳裡，不管奴隸幹完活有多累，就是得跳舞。

「跳吧，你們這些該死的奴隸，跳吧！」伊普司喊道。

這裡沒有讓你喘息的時間，誰要是敢停下來喘口氣，鞭子已經伺候在旁了。這會一直持續到天快亮，而等隔天天一亮，大夥都得去田裡幹活。當天傍晚，就算棉花的採收量不足，鞭子照打不誤。若要說有什麼不同的話，那就是在深夜的跳舞之後，伊普司的脾氣會更加乖戾。

第十章　聖誕節

P. 60

伊普司在霍夫包待了兩年，這時他也掙夠了錢，可以在河口的對岸買一塊自己的農場。一八四五年，他搬了過去，帶上九個奴隸，包括我。在往後的八年裡，我就都和這些人在一起。

一八四五年，在伊普司新農場的第一年，這一帶遭受蟲害，棉花沒有收成。奴隸們沒有工作可做，我們便被帶到墨西哥灣那裡去砍甘蔗，等工作完成了，再帶我們回來。不過，接下來連續三年，在採收甘蔗的季節時，伊普司以一天一塊錢的價錢，把我外租出去，這個價碼對他來說很划算。

第二年的夏天，我找到了一個改善飲食的方法。我們奴隸每個星期會配給煙燻培根和玉蜀黍，可是在夏天，肉往往長滿蛆，根本不能吃。

P. 61

夜裡，有些奴隸會去河灣獵捕浣熊或是其他的野生動物，給自己補一些肉食。然而一整天工作下來，要再去獵食，談何容易。不過因為我的小木屋就在河灣附近，我就發明了一個很好用的魚罟，從此以後，我和朋友們都有新鮮的魚可以吃了。

奴隸唯一可以不用工作的放假時間，就是在聖誕節。伊普司給我們三天的假，這是吃喝玩樂的歡樂時光，人人會把煩惱拋諸腦後，奴隸可以盡情享受一點點有限的自由。

農場主會給自己和鄰近農場的奴隸，準備一份聖誕大餐，每年換一次東道主。參加的人大概有四百人，大家都會穿上自己最好的衣服。桌席會擺在戶外，我們可以享用雞肉、鴨肉、火雞肉、豬肉和蔬菜。此外，還有桃子醬餅乾、派餅和其他的甜點。長桌子上，男的坐一邊，女的坐一邊，大家一邊吃，一邊說話打趣，歡笑聲不斷。

P. 62

大餐之後，接著是聖誕舞會，我負責拉小提琴。真的，若不是有我心愛的小提琴，我真不曉得要怎麼熬過被奴役的這些歲月。這表示我可以在農場主宅邸的宴會上演奏，這讓我可以掙些錢；此外，在我或悲或喜的時刻裡，它也是我的知己。聖誕節怎麼說都是一個很特別的日子，我可以幫奴隸朋友們助興，在星光下盡情跳舞。

過完耶誕節，會發通行證給奴隸，大家可以在限定的距離內，自由走動。因為不用工作、不用擔心吃鞭子，奴隸們的神情和舉止，整個都不一樣了。大家會去找舊識，在這一帶四處遊走。這段時間，也是奴隸結婚的旺季，只要雙方的奴隸主同意，就可以成親。

聖誕節

- 比較一下你的聖誕節和奴隸們的聖誕節。

第十一章　信件

P. 63

除了砍甘蔗的季節，我都在伊普司的農場工作。他算是小園主，不需要像福特老爺那樣，有查賓來當監工。監工會騎著馬到田裡，身上帶著鞭子、手槍、刀子，還會跟著幾隻狗。要夠冷血、夠殘忍、夠狠心，才配當一個監工。監工的職責是讓收成良好，至於要用多少的痛苦去換取，並不重要。

監工下面會有一、兩個工頭，由黑奴擔任，他們除了有自己的工作要完成，還要被迫拿鞭子管理所負責的其他奴隸。他們會把鞭子盤在脖子上，如果不好好使用鞭子，那他們自己就要挨鞭子。

伊普司搬到新農場後，要我當工頭，監工的工作則由伊普司自己來做。

P. 64

只要伊普司在場，我就不敢好聲好氣。但就算伊普司沒有跟我們在一起，他也能在某個隱密地地方監看情況。要是有誰老是工作不賣力，伊普司就會鞭打，而我如果縱容，就要連帶吃鞭子。他要是看我常常抽鞭子，就會誇獎我。

不過，在我擔任監工的八年歲月裡，我學會了如何精準地抽鞭子，讓鞭子貼近背部，卻不會碰到。我的朋友們也知道要裝出一副痛得扭動尖叫的樣子，好讓伊普司相信他們挨了鞭子。

有一次，伊普司問我會不會讀書寫字，我跟他說我會。他就說，要是讓他撞見我帶著書本或筆墨，就會給我吃一百下鞭子。

「我買奴隸，是要來幹活用的，不是要讓他受教育。」他說。

我的最大目標，始終是設法收到友人或家人的來信，但這事簡直是不可能的。我無法弄到筆墨和紙，而且沒有通行證，沒有奴隸能夠出得了農場。要是沒有奴隸主的指示，郵局局長也不可能給奴隸送信。這我花了九年的時間，才找到一個機會。

P. 65

伊普司去紐奧良賣棉花，太太派我去洪司市採購一些物品，包括買紙。我從中取了一張紙，藏在我睡覺的木板下面。我又拿楓樹皮來煮，當墨汁用，再拿一根鴨毛來當筆。

夜裡，我寫了一封長長的信，要寄給沙地山的一位老友，我跟他說明我的處境，請他援助我獲得自由。這封信我留在身邊很久的時間，我一直在想辦法要如何安全地把信送到郵局。

通訊來往

- 你如何和別人通訊來往？
- 你多常使用這種通訊方式？

曾經有一個叫昂史比的人，他想來找監工的工作，待在伊普司這裡住了幾天。我找各種方式跟他談話，當他說他常去十八哩外的馬克市時，我想他或許可以幫我寄信。

P. 66

一天晚上，我來到昂史比睡覺的地

方，請求他幫忙。我央求他，就算他不能幫我寄信，也不要跟伊普司說。他表示，他可以幫我寄信，也會保守這個祕密。

然而，兩天後，我看到昂史比和伊普司聊了好一段時間。當天晚上，伊普司的手上提著鞭子，走進我的小屋裡來。

他開口說道：「好小子，看來我有一個聰明的奴隸，會寫信找人寄出去。我納悶這人是誰呀？」

「伊普司老爺，我不知道你在說什麼。」我回答。

「你不是找了昂史比說了這件事？」他問。

「我絕對沒有，我跟他說話都不超過三個字的。」我回答。

「昂史比說，你把他吵醒，要他幫你帶封信去馬克市。」

「老爺，沒有這回事。我沒有墨水，也沒有紙，怎麼可能寫信？我也沒有人可以寫信，我在這世上無親無故。大家都說昂史比是個滿口謊言的酒鬼，他的話沒人會信。他的詭計是很清楚的，他想要當你的監工，就編出這樣的故事來唬弄，那你就會雇用他來監督我們了。」我回答。

「哎呀，普雷特，我想你講的沒錯，昂史比一定以為我是笨蛋，才會來這裡跟我胡扯了這樣的事。」

P. 67

背叛

- 你曾被你以為可以相信的人所背叛過嗎？
- 你當時的感覺如何？
- 當時被背叛之後的結果是什麼？和夥伴分享。

伊普司走出小屋。我一陣心碎，立刻就把信燒掉。我不想冒任何的風險。

第二天，昂史比被攆出伊普司的農場，我鬆了好大一口氣。

我不知道自己如何可以被營救出來。我感到自己逐漸老去，再過了幾年的辛勞苦役和悲慘歲月，我的命運就是死去，被人所遺忘。獲救的希望是我唯一的安慰，但如今這個希望是如此渺茫。我準備好活在黑暗之中，一直到生命的盡頭。

第十二章　貝斯

P. 69

一八五二年六月，伊普司要我去協助木工艾利先生蓋房子。在艾利的手下當中，有一個叫貝斯的人，是他幫我獲得了自由。

貝斯是一個年約四十五歲的單身漢，住在馬克市，他每兩個星期會回家一次。他是一個仁慈且開明的人，隨時準備好談論從政治到宗教的話題。

這一天，貝斯和伊普司爭論著奴役的問題，我頗具興味地聆聽著。

「伊普司，這是大錯特錯的，就算我是大富翁，我一個奴隸也不會有。你有什麼權利可以擁有黑奴？」貝斯說。

「什麼權利？」伊普司笑道：「就因為是我買來的呀！」

「你當然是買來的，法律說你可以這麼做，但那樣的法律是錯的。」貝斯說道：「我問你，白人和黑人有什麼不一樣？」

P. 70

「徹徹底底不一樣。你倒不如問白人和猴子有什麼不一樣！」伊普司回答。

「但是，伊普司，《獨立宣言》裡不是說人人生而平等嗎？」貝斯繼續說道。

「是沒錯，但那是說所有『人』，而不是說奴隸和猴子。」伊普司答道。

所有人類

- 請使用網路來找《獨立宣言》的資料。

「在白人之中，也有猴子。」貝斯平靜地說道：「這些奴隸是人類，他們被禁止接受教育，而你有書、有報紙，愛上哪兒就上哪兒，但你的奴隸卻沒有這樣的特權。你抓到誰在看書，你就鞭打他。這種情況一代又一代的延續下去。奴役是罪惡，應該廢除。」

P. 71

說到這裡，伊普司站起來離開，不過在這之後，還是有類似的談話。

我決定，貝斯就是那個人，我要跟他說出自己的情況。有一天，我們單獨一起工作，於是我準備冒險碰運氣。

「貝斯老爺，你打哪兒來的？」我開始說道。

他回答：「怎麼，普雷特，就算我跟你說，你也不會知道。我是在加拿大出生的。」

「我去過加拿大。」我說：「我到過蒙特利爾、金斯頓、皇后鎮。我還去過紐約州，到過水牛城、羅徹斯特和奧爾巴尼。」

「那你怎麼會在這裡？你是誰？」他問。

我跟他說，這說來話長，而伊普司很快就會回來。我請他過了半夜再來這房子，跟我相見。他允諾我，會對我所說的一切守口如瓶。

我們依約碰了面，我跟他說了我的身世。我請求他寫信給我北方的友人，幫助我重獲自由。他答應了我的事，但也提醒我說，他幫我通報，會有性命的危險。接著，我們做了策畫。

P. 73

第二天夜裡，我們又碰了面。我託他寫信要寄去的姓名和住址，他記下了，接著他說：「你離開薩拉托加已經好幾年了，這些人可能已經過世，或是搬家了。你說你在紐約的海關辦過文件，那裡或許還留有你的紀錄，所以我想也一併寫信給他們會比較好。」

我同意他的想法，並說他要是能幫我獲得自由，我不勝感激。他說，他孑然一身，沒有家庭，他很高興能全力幫我爭取自由。

貝斯下一次從馬克市返回之後，他跟我說，他星期日的時間都在寫信，一封要寄給紐約海關的馬文法官，另外一封

要一併寄給帕克先生和派瑞先生，而後面寄出的這一封信，讓我最終獲釋。

從這時候開始，每次貝斯只要去馬克市，我就非常的興奮，但只要他空手回來，我就又很失望。

十個星期過去了，房子也已經蓋好。在貝斯要離開前的那個夜晚，我徹底的絕望了。他說，他在聖誕節的前一天會回來，他想繼續幫我尋回自由。

貝斯信守了他的諾言，他在聖誕節的前夕回來了。伊普司帶他到大宅裡，他就在那裡過夜。清晨一大早，他來到了我的小屋。

P. 74

「普雷特，還沒有信寄來。」他說。

聽到這消息，我的心一沉。

「哦，請再寫信去，貝斯老爺。」我喊道：「我會把我知道的名字都告訴你。」

貝斯說：「這不行，馬克市的郵局會起疑的。」他繼續說道：「不過，我決定親自去一趟薩拉托加。我在三、四月之前還有一些工作要完成，之後我就有足夠的盤纏去那裡了。」

我很難相信他的話。

「我現在得走了，伊普司很快就會起床，我不能被人看到我在這裡。但是我很快就會再過來，在這之前，好好回想你在薩拉托加和沙地山所認識的人，我會把他們的名字抄下來，這樣我去北方時就知道要去找誰了。提起精神吧，我和你同在。」

P. 75

一八五三年一月三日，我們外出幹活。這是一個寒冷的早上，在這個地方，這樣的天氣不常見。

伊普司走出來，竟沒有帶上鞭子——這實在是太不尋常了。有一個奴隸竟膽敢說他的手指太凍了，採收的動作快不起來。伊普司咒罵自己沒有皮鞭可以抽打他，就騎著馬去拿鞭子。

他離開之後，我們注意到有一輛馬車迅速地駛向宅邸。接著，我們看到有兩個人穿越棉花田，走向我們。

第十三章　寄回家的信

P. 76

在繼續故事之前，容我回溯一下，說明貝斯在一八五二年八月十五日寄出三封信之後，發生了什麼事。

寄給帕克和派瑞的信，在九月初寄給了薩拉托加。帕克和派瑞把信轉寄給我的妻子安妮，安妮立刻去沙地山尋求亨利 ·B· 諾薩普的意見。

亨利 ·B· 諾薩普發現，從一八四〇年以來，有一個法令授權州政府當局可以釋放被綁架到他州當奴隸的人。為了達到這個目的，要出示兩項證明：第一，當事人是自由公民；第二，當事人遭受非法奴役。

收集了文件之後，委派了亨利 ·B· 諾薩普處理一切事宜。

十二月十四日，諾薩普啟程離開。他前往華盛頓，拿到進一步的文件，要呈給路易斯安那州當局。接著，他南下到馬克市，於一八五三年一月一日上午九點抵達。他把文件呈給馬克市法院一位叫做約翰 ·P· 瓦迪爾的律師。

P. 77

不過，貝斯寫的信是使用我的真名所羅門 · 諾薩普，人們不知道有叫這個名字的奴隸，只知道有普雷特。因此，要尋找我，看來是很不可能。

因為那天是星期日，他們決定隔天離開返家，諾薩普和瓦迪爾有時間待在一起。他們聊到彼此對北方蓄奴的不同態度。

諾薩普問瓦迪爾，在馬克市，他有沒

有聽過有人的言論是反對奴役的。瓦迪爾回答，只有一個人，就是貝斯。他之後閃過一個念頭，便又瞧了瞧那封寄到薩拉托加的信。

「這是貝斯的筆跡！」瓦迪爾喊道：「貝斯這個人可以跟我們說所羅門 · 諾薩普的下落。」

他們找到了貝斯，貝斯當時正在河邊等著搭船，準備離開兩個星期。他們恰巧在他上船之前找到了他。

諾薩普說：「貝斯先生，我從紐約來，要尋找寫信提到所羅門 · 諾薩普的人。如果你知道這個人，請告訴我可以去哪兒找他。我向你保證，決不向任何人透露你的資料。」

P. 79

「就是我寫那封信的。」貝斯回答：「如

果你是要來營救所羅門·諾薩普，那我很高興見到你。他是愛德恩·伊普司的奴隸，那是洪司市附近的一個農場主。大家是叫他普雷特。」

貝斯接著說了去那裡的最快路線。

諾薩普還有一些必要的文件得完成。瓦迪爾風聞貝斯離開了鎮上，而且有謠言流傳說，下榻旅館的一個陌生人（諾薩普）和瓦迪爾，正奔走著要釋放伊普司的一個奴隸，於是情況突然變得緊急起來了。

瓦迪爾擔心，風聲可能很快就會傳到伊普司那裡，所以他們在午夜後得到了法官的簽名文件後，載著警長和諾薩普先生的馬車當晚立刻啟程。

他們決定，在讓我和諾薩普談話之前，先由警長來詢問我的個人資料。要是我的回答無誤，那這些證明就完全足以採信了。

第十四章　我的獲救

P. 80

現在，回到之前說到的那兩個人，他們穿越田地，朝我們走過來。

警長走向我，說道：「你就是普雷特，對嗎？」

「是的，老爺。」我回答。

「你認識那個人嗎？」他一邊問，一邊朝諾薩普指過去。

我大聲地喊道：「亨利·B·諾薩普！謝天謝地！」

我立刻要朝他走去，但警長攔住了我。

「等等，除了普雷特，你還有別的名字嗎？」他說。

「所羅門·諾薩普，老爺。」我回答。

「你有家人嗎？」他又問。

「我『以前』有一個妻子，還有三個孩子，伊麗莎白、瑪格麗特和亞倫佐。」

「那位先生住在哪裡？」他再度指著諾薩普，問我道。

「他住在紐約州華盛頓的沙地山。」我如此回答。

P. 81

我推開警長，向我這位老朋友走過去。我抓著他的雙手，開始哭了起來。

「所羅門，見到你我真高興。」諾薩普說。

我想回話，但我情緒激動得無法言語。

奴隸們站在那裡，目瞪口呆地看著。

這些年的歲月，我都與他們一起共度，大家承受著同樣的苦難。他們分享著我的悲傷，還有些許的快樂，但他們沒有人知道我的任何身世。

「把棉花袋放下吧，你採收棉花的日子已經結束了。」諾薩普說道。

伊普司和警長握了握手，警長向他介紹了諾薩普先生，他便請他們進到屋子裡。

等我進到屋子時，桌子上擺滿了資料，諾薩普正在閱讀一份文件，伊普司這時打斷了他。

「普雷特，你認識這個人嗎？」

「老爺，我認識。打我有記憶以來，我就知道這個人了。」我回答道。

「他住在哪裡？」

「紐約州。」

P. 83

「你也住過那裡？」

「是的，老爺，我是在那裡土生土長的。」

「這麼說，你以前是自由之身囉！我買你的時候，你怎麼不告訴我？」他嚷道。

我回答道：「伊普司老爺，這您沒問過。而且，我以前對綁架我的人說我是自由之身，結果差一點死在他的鞭子下。」

「看來，是有人幫你寫了信，那人是誰？」他查問道。

「也許是我自己寫的。」我回答道。

「你沒到過馬克市的郵局，這點我知道。」

伊普司就是想問清楚，但我就是不說。他開始放話威脅這位不明人士，揚言要是被他查出來是誰，就要取了他的性命。

我走到院子裡，遇到了伊普司太太。她說，她很難過要失去我，沒有任何奴隸比得上我，我幫上很多忙，還會為她拉小提琴。講到最後，她流下了眼淚。

我向奴隸朋友們、伊普司老爺和太太道別，然後轉身走向馬車，諾薩普和警長在那邊等著我。

P. 85

一月四日星期二，伊普司、他的律師（一位泰勒先生）、諾薩普、瓦迪爾、法官、警長，這些人在馬克市一個房間裡會面。諾薩普先生陳述了我的背景資料，出示所有必要的文件，警長並描述了在棉花田見到我的情景。他們也問了我很多問題。

最後，泰勒先生向他的委託人說，他確信這些證據沒有問題。他們便擬了一份文件並簽署，宣示伊普司接受我的自由權利，並將我正式交給紐約州當局。

我和諾薩普先生隨即去趕搭下一艘汽船，離開那裡。

很快地，我們沿著紅河順流而下。那麼多年以前，逆河而上被帶走時，我是如此鬱悒。如今，我自由了。在我們離開此地之際，我細細思索了過去的這些歲月。

十年來，我為伊普司工作，沒有酬勞。十年無止無休的工作，給伊普司帶來更多的財富。十年來，我跟他說話時，眼神要往下看，頭要低下來，這是奴隸該有的舉止。最後，我沒有從他那裡換到什麼，除了不當的凌虐和鞭打。

P. 86

他是個沒有仁慈或正義之心的人，他只有粗暴的精力，交伴著未受教育的心靈和貪婪的人性。伊普司被說是「奴隸毀滅者」，他摧毀奴隸心靈的能耐，是出了名的。他以這樣的名聲自豪，他不認為黑人是人類，而是像騾或狗那樣，是一項活物財產。

奴隸毀滅者

- 伊普司為何會有這個名號，請列出原因。
- 你覺得伊普司這個人如何？和夥伴分享。

第十五章　返鄉

P. 87

我們在紐奧良停留了兩天，以便拿到官方授予的合法通行證，上面會說明亨利 ·B· 諾薩普有權帶我經過南部各州，前往紐約州。

之後，我們搭火車前往查爾斯頓。我們在查爾斯頓要搭汽船時，海關官員問諾薩普先生，怎麼不去註冊自己的奴隸。他回答，他沒有奴隸，並說明了情況。我擔心他們還是會找我麻煩，但他們把我們放行了。一八五三年一月十七日，我們抵達了華盛頓。

歸鄉之旅

- 查看第 30 頁的地圖，或是上網看地圖，追蹤一下所羅門返家的路程。
- 請列出所羅門搭了哪些不同的交通工具，才回到了家。

P. 88

我們一到華盛頓，就開始調查我被綁架一事。沒有任何門路可以查出布朗和漢彌頓這兩個人的資料，不過，我們發現伯奇和拉德本還住在華盛頓。我們立刻向警方提出控訴，控告詹姆斯 ·H· 伯奇綁架我，把我賣去當奴隸。

伯奇立刻遭到逮捕。一月十八日，當著法院法官的面，開庭審訊了好一段時間，各方證人都來了。在庭上，有兩個伯奇的證人，他們說伯奇是合法向我的主人買下我的，是我和布朗、漢彌頓聯合起來，要誣陷伯奇的。

因為我的膚色的關係，他們不允許我以證人的身分發言，或是陳述我自己的說詞。

最後，經過調查，在伯奇一八四一年的帳冊中，並沒有找到什麼名字與買賣我有關。根據這一點，法院就判定伯奇是在清白誠實的情況下買下我的，所以無罪釋放。

P. 90

我不知道人們會是如何相信我十二年前在華盛頓所經歷過的事。我要是像伯奇所說的那樣，故意誣陷他，那我又何苦回來華盛頓，並要求在判決之前一定要開庭審訊？

我希望大家都能夠知道真相，但早知如此，我或許應該直接回家，而不要在華盛頓作停留，想把綁架我的人繩之以法。

最起碼，我在此地講述了我的經歷，能把事實講出來，最後的公道自在人心。

我和諾薩普離開華盛頓。一月二十二日上午，我前往格蘭弗斯，安和孩子們住在那裡。

我們相見時的情緒，筆墨難以形容。安和伊麗莎白摟著我哭泣。而我離開時，瑪格麗特才七歲大，她已經不記得我了。而今，她已經嫁作人婦，有一個小兒子。

我們稍微平靜了之後，便圍坐在爐火旁，開始細說過去這十二年來所發生的太多事情。

P. 91

在此，我的故事落幕了。對於奴役的事，我不予評論。看了這本書的人們，會有自己的心得。其他州的情況如何，我不了解。但我可以坦誠地說，對於我待過的各州的奴役狀況，我切切實實地描述出來，沒有杜撰，沒有誇大。我確信，有數百個自由之身的人遭受綁架，被賣去當奴隸，而在此時此刻，他們仍在德州和路易斯安那州的農場裡，過著暗無天日的生活。

我的發言只能代表我自己，說出我自己所遭遇的苦難。我充滿感激，能夠重返幸福與自由的生活。

此時，我只希望能夠過著美好而簡單的生活，然後在我父親現在長眠的地方安息。

ANSWER KEY

Before Reading

Pages 8-9

1 abolish, chains, owner, work, punishment, legal property
2 a) legal property
b) chains
c) punishment
d) owner
3 a) 4 b) 3 c) 1 d) 2

Pages 10-11

4 a) steamboat
b) sailing ship
c) wagon
d) on foot
5 a) 2 b) 4 c) 3 d) 1
6 a) lived quite well
b) a hard worker
c) a family man

Pages 12-13

7 a) T b) T c) F d) F e) T
8 a) 5 b) 4 c) 3 d) 2 e) 1
9 a) Ford: good
b) Tibeats: bad
c) Epps: bad
10 a) religious, master, lucky
b) bad-tempered, opposite
c) spoke, manners, drank, cunning

Page 26

- Brown and Hamilton kidnapped Solomon.

Page 27

- yard, horse blankets, pen

Page 41

- He tells Tibeats that Solomon is still William Ford's property and his duty is to protect him.

Page 55

- pick cotton, feed the mules and pigs, cut wood, make a fire, and cook supper and lunch

Page 86

- Epps had no sense of kindness.
He destroyed the spirit of his slaves.
He saw the slave as a piece of property, like a dog.

Page 87

- Solomon uses a train and a steamboat.

After Reading

Pages 94-95

8 a) F b) F c) F d) T
e) F f) T g) T h) T

9 a) He was freed by the Northup family.
b) He was born a free man.
c) His real name was Solomon Northup.
e) His first owner was the only reasonably kind person.

10 a) Hamilton and Brown.
b) Free papers.
c) New York and Washington.
d) New Orleans.
e) Arthur.
f) $1,000.

11 a) 3 b) 1 c) 4 d) 2

Pages 96-97

13 a) 3 b) 1 c) 4 d) 2

14 Christmas.

15 a) freed
b) debt
c) satisfied
d) hang
e) cruel
f) drunk, whipping
g) helped
h) freedom

Pages 98-99

17 b)

18 a) 2
b) 2

19 a) It is Solomon himself.
b) He is saying slaves are the same as monkeys, i.e. animals.
c) Chapin is trying to convince Tibeats that slaves also have certain rights.

Pages 100-101

20 a) 4 b) 7 c) 1 d) 6
e) 2 f) 5 g) 8 h) 3

21 a) dawn
b) dusk
c) 15 minutes
d) 85 kilos
e) a whipping
f) corn and bacon
g) feed mules and pigs, cut wood, and cook super and lunch for the next day
h) after midnight

22 b, e, f

23 a) some white people behave like monkeys/animals
b) how we live, our brain, our rules and laws

Test

Pages 102-103

25 *(connected to slavery)* owner, slave dealer, master, whipping, punishment, prisoner
(against slavery) abolish/abolitionist, freedom, free man, liberty, illegal, equality

26 a) free, free
b) freedom
c) free
d) free
e) freedom

27 a) there was a law for the slave as well as for the white man
b) he wouldn't own a slave if he were a millionaire
c) "Please don't tell Epps if you can't post the letter."
d) why he was there and who he was

28 a) 2 b) 3 c) 4 d) 1

29 a) in twos
b) in no fit state
c) in chains
d) in the wrong

Pages 104-105

1 a) 2 b) 2 c) 2 d) 1
2 a) 2 b) 3 c) 4 d) 2 e) 1
3 a) 3 b) 2 c) 4 d) 1

國家圖書館出版品預行編目資料

自由之心：為奴十二年 / Solomon Northup 著 ; David A. Hill 改寫 ; 安卡斯 譯. 一初版. 一[臺北市]：寂天文化, 2016.4 面； 公分. 中英對照; 譯自：Twelve years a slave

ISBN 978-986-318-442-3 (平裝附光碟片)
1. 英語 2. 讀本

805.18 105003621

原著 _ Solomon Northup
改寫 _ David A. Hill
譯者 _ 安卡斯
校對 _ 陳慧莉
製程管理 _ 洪巧玲
出版者 _ 寂天文化事業股份有限公司
電話 _ +886-2-2365-9739
傳真 _ +886-2-2365-9835
網址 _ www.icosmos.com.tw
讀者服務 _ onlineservice@icosmos.com.tw
出版日期 _ 2016年4月 初版一刷（250101）
郵撥帳號 _ 1998620-0 寂天文化事業股份有限公司